$\mathcal{A}$ CANDLELIGHT ROMANCE

CANDLELIGHT ROMANCES

FAREWELL TO ALEXANDRIA

Suzanne Roberts

A CANDLELIGHT ROMANCE

Published by
Dell Publishing Co., Inc.
1 Dag Hammarskjold Plaza
New York, New York 10017

Dell ® TM 681510, Dell Publishing Co., Inc.

ISBN 0-440-12587-1

Printed in the United States of America
First printing—February 1980

One

When the newest of the worldwide Hotel Teresas was finished, a towering white structure overlooking the brilliantly blue sea in the city of Alexandria, they came, twelve of them. Included were the founder and chief stockholder and an American doctor, since the hotels' owner did not seem to trust foreign doctors.

The flight originated at Chicago's O'Hare Airport, going on to Kennedy in New York, where two employees of the New York Hotel Teresa were met and greeted by Mr. Michael Mulvaney, the sixty-year-old owner of that vast hotel empire that had made him heir to a fortune that his grandfather had acquired when he came over from County Wicklow, Ireland.

Next the huge luxury jet made its way to Heathrow in London, where the lucky employee there, voted by the staff of Hotel Teresa employees to be "most liked," got on the plane, along with the manager of the London hotel.

So finally they were all on board, the girl from Chicago's Hotel Teresa, the girl from London, the managers, vice-presidents, the doctor, and of course, old Mr. Mulvaney himself.

They stopped in Paris, landing at Orly to have lunch, then they went on to Cairo, where they were met by a smiling manager. Their final stop was Alexandria, where the beautiful, brand-new Hotel Teresa had just been opened to guests.

Lori Coleman, from Chicago, had no way of knowing

that her life was about to change, that in Alexandria, old city of many wars, countless broken dreams and poets' praises, she would find another self inside her; it would be as if she became someone else.

She worked in the huge, sterile kitchen of Chicago's towering Teresa, a member of a carefully chosen kitchen staff of well over a hundred cooks and bakers. Before she had studied home economics at the university at nights for two years, working daytime for her uncle in his café. Lori had decided to make a change, however, when her fiancé's body was found at last in Vietnam, and the long waiting and hoping were finally over.

At the hotel she had been screened as carefully as if she were applying for some high-powered government job. She was hired finally and assigned to a staff of bakers who did nothing but mix and frost the fancy desserts that graced the tables of some of the most famous—and infamous—people in the world.

When told she had been chosen in the annual contest to make a trip somewhere with the owner and various managers of the hotels, Lori had been at first numbed with shock and then undecided as to whether or not she should go. She came from a large, conservative family, where girls lived at home until they married and boys were expected either to work and go to the university or work and help out at home. Traveling was considered unnecessary for the most part. Lori knew the objections a trip abroad, even a free one, would bring from her family, and she was right. They had been horror-struck at the idea of her going to Egypt.

But finally something had urged her to accept in spite of her family's disapproval. The trip was nearly four months in the planning and, until they actually arrived in Alexandria, went without a hitch.

There the limos that were scheduled to pick them up simply were not at the airport. Michael Mulvaney, not used to having his plans go wrong, made phone calls and came back to the VIP lounge, where everyone waited, with his face red and his blue eyes flashing rage.

A mix-up about arrival times . . . they were on their way but there had been some sort of mishap, a flat tire. . . .

Lori, sitting in one of the deep leather chairs, was simply too weary to care much. She scarcely paid attention when a uniformed chauffeur came into the room, hat in hand, and spoke quietly to Mr. Mulvaney. The aging Irishman nodded, peered outside, shook hands with the chauffeur, and then made his announcement to the entire group that sat waiting:

"Ladies and gentlemen, we have been rescued by a generous resident of Alexandria who wishes us to go to our hotel. In view of the jet lag some of the ladies seem to be suffering from, I suggest we all go to the hotel at once and our luggage can be picked up and delivered when and if the hotel's cars ever manage to get on the road. Come along, ladies."

The waiting car was a long, silver-colored Rolls. There were pull-down side seats, and by using those and seating two people in the front with the driver, everyone managed to get in, although it was a tight squeeze. The car, however, was so luxurious that even squeezed in, it was quite comfortable.

As they drove off, Lori had a brief glimpse of the car's owner, a man named Paul Kardett, according to her boss. Kardett walked across the somewhat misty runway near the tower, along with a young woman who seemed to be

7

wearing white slacks and a matching top. Then he helped her into a small sea plane and got in himself. As Lori watched, the little blue and silver plane took off, flying close over the Rolls, which was now going along the highway toward town. As the plane reached the edge of the sea, it dipped first one wing then the other in a gesture of salute.

At the new hotel Julia, from London, and Lori were to share a room, but once in the room they said very little. Julia murmured something inaudible, then crawled into her bed with her clothes still on.

Only Lori remained awake, sitting by the sliding glass doors that led out to a small balcony. It was early still; most of the city slept. She sipped strong tea brought by a smiling Arab boy who spoke no English, and finally, as if drawn by something beyond her control, she quietly slid open the glass window and stepped out onto the little balcony.

All around her was the pungent essence of lemons. The morning air seemed to be full of sweet-smelling dust, pinkish brick dust it was, filtering up from clean streets that had been slaked with water. The air from the sea lightly varnished everything; the day's heat had not yet begun, so that standing there high above the ancient city Lori felt only a kind of lemon-sweet, damp, and cool breeze.

She was becoming enchanted without understanding why or caring in the least bit. Far from home, away from home for the first time, Lori saw the old city unroll itself before her like some kind of ancient seductress, showing with a kind of pride all its crushing beauty.

To her right were little shops, protected from the sun by ragged awnings. The merchants were beginning to open up, piling their goods outside in racks—live quail, honeycombs, mirrors that caught the sunlight, fruit stalls with warm gold oranges and huge lemons, and finally the pottery shops, with long strings of blue jade beads, rings, and ankle bracelets.

In one of the nearby cafés, someone turned on a radio— news of the peace talks and then loud, tinny-sounding music. People began coming out onto the street, Ethiopians in white turbans, Sudanese and Lebanese, Moslem women hidden behind veils. An American car sped down the street recklessly, followed by a man on a camel and another leading a donkey.

Lori let out her breath. She felt marvelous for some reason. She undressed, crawled into her bed, closed her grateful eyes, and slept.

She woke up to brilliant sunlight flooding the room; a fresh tea tray was on the low table near the glass patio doors leading to the balcony. Lori sat up, feeling a bit groggy from her long sleep, pushed back her honey-brown hair from her face, and looked around the room for Julia. The opposite twin bed was empty and unmade, and from the bathroom came the somehow sane and cheerful sound of a running shower.

On the flight over from London it had seemed to Lori that Julia was perhaps a bit unfriendly, but now, with a large blue towel wrapped around her wet hair, wearing a scruffy-looking robe, her feet bare, Julia suddenly seemed very different.

"Good afternoon," she said pleasantly to Lori, her accent British and casual. "Glad to see you've survived the jet lag. I hope the tea isn't cold; they brought it when you were still out like a light." She grinned. "That's an American expression, isn't it?"

Lori smiled back. "The tea is fine," she said. "I hope I haven't slept through anything important. Have I?"

Julia began brushing her damp, expertly bleached long

hair. She was the typically beautiful English girl—naturally blonde, with only a bit of help to make her pale hair brighter, steady gray eyes, and lovely white skin.

"Only a stupid meeting this morning, early, to get us acquainted with the staff here, but I don't think it mattered that neither of us showed up." Her gray eyes narrowed. "Do you mind if I'm completely honest with you, Luv?"

"Why—no," Lori said, a little startled. "I want you to be."

"If I didn't have some reason for coming here other than seeing the sights, I'd be back in London right now, enjoying the spring weather. I don't know about you, my dear, but I look upon this trip as an unexpected way to find myself a very rich husband, before I grow too old for anyone to want me."

"I see," Lori said, trying not to look surprised. Her own reasons for having come were so vastly different that she suddenly felt the hoped-for friendship with Julia might never get off the ground. "Well, good luck." She began taking things out of her suitcase. "You're very pretty; you shouldn't have any trouble." She wanted no bad feelings, no petty jealousies, no female nastiness. That morning, when she stood on the balcony, she had felt an odd sense of peace, even though Egypt had no real peace as yet. But there had been a dim sense of history, or perhaps it had only been that she was far away from the pressures and memories of home for the first time.

At any rate it was something she could not explain to this practical British girl, at least not yet, not until they had become friends—if they did.

"What I'm trying to say," Julia told her, "is that I'd appreciate it if you don't interfere with my reason for being here, and I'll do the same for you. You're very beautiful—and I wouldn't be at all surprised or annoyed if you were

10

to admit that you've come to find a rich husband, too." She poured two cups of tea and carried one to Lori. "Have you?"

"No."

There was a small silence; calm gray eyes looked into Lori's green-gold ones.

"Do you know," Julia said finally, "I believe you! I suppose that means you've someone special back home."

So the moment had come. Lori sipped the tea and kept her eyes on the blue sea, beyond the glass doors.

"There was. He died in Vietnam, in the war. But we . . . we didn't know for sure until the winter before last, when they found the plane in the jungle."

For an instant Julia's eyes softened, then she turned back to her hair-brushing.

"That war's been over for a long while. You must have been very young."

"When he left, you mean? I was seventeen, just out of high school. Tommy was four years older. He'd been a friend of my brother's. We were very close," Lori said quietly. "We grew up together. Somehow, getting married to him seemed like something that would be easy and—and right, for both of us."

"Sometimes," Julia said, "we have to do an about face, Luv. You know what they say about the best laid plans of mice and men. Now, as for me, I've been looking for Mr. Right ever since I was seventeen, but in my case, nobody died—I just kept running into poor chappies who were never going to be anything but poor. I'm twenty-four now, and it's high time I married. How old are you, by the way?"

"Twenty-four. And I'm not the least bit interested in marriage, thank you."

Julia grinned. "Good. Look, why don't we do some sightseeing before we get our orders for the day? There's to be a party or something later, at the French Consulate."

Lori was glad the talk had turned to happier things. "I'd love it. I don't suppose they'd send up coffee if we asked, do you?"

"I'll order it. You Americans and your coffee!"

They liked each other, and although each girl was a bit wary, they had a beginning, and they both knew it. Or maybe it was just being in this old city that made Lori feel as if she had found someone to talk to, at last.

The coffee came, with rich cakes on yet another silver tray, but the proposed shopping trip was curtailed by a phone call from Lori's immediate boss, the manager of the Hotel Teresa in Chicago.

"This is Frank Corita, Miss Coleman. Where were you this morning at the staff meeting?"

"Asleep. I'm sorry, but I was exhausted."

"Kindly be ready early for the party at the Consulate. We don't want Chicago to look bad, you know."

"Of course not, Mr. Corita."

"Then be ready in an hour."

Lori hung up and looked at Julia. "No sightseeing, I'm afraid. At least not right now."

So while Julia pressed a striking cocktail dress, Lori soaked in the beautiful pink and white tub. Someone had thoughtfully put bath crystals, scented with roses, on the tub and there were bars of soap from Paris wrapped in silver paper.

Suddenly Julia pounded on the bathroom door. "I think you'd better come and see something."

Lori reached for her robe, getting into it still wet. Then she opened the door and stared.

Flowers. Dozens and dozens of them, roses in pale cream and yellow, jasmine heavy with its perfume, lush desert flowers with pale leaves and slender petals. There were vases and baskets and pots and slender jars of them; they seemed to fill the room.

"Is there a card?"

"I haven't found one," Julia said, still looking behind flowers, into pots, into baskets. "Here—here it is. They must have cost a fortune!"

Both girls peeked at it. There was a crest on top, engraved in gold, and the paper was both formal and heavy. The note was handwritten in black ink and addressed to Lori: "Welcome to Alexandria, Miss Coleman." And it was signed simply, "Paul Kardett."

Lori's eyes widened. "Paul Kardett? Who—"

"The man at the airport, remember? The one who loaned his Rolls, so we could come to the hotel!"

"Oh," Lori said, not really interested. "Him. Yes; I noticed him. He took off in a little plane with a girl."

"Girl or not, he's obviously taken with you, duckie. He must have gone to a bit of trouble to find out who you were. You ought to be highly flattered, you know. I certainly would be!"

Lori frowned. "But—I didn't even think he'd seen me!"

"Oh, he saw us, all right. Remember when we were all being escorted to the VIP lounge, and Mr. Mulvaney was acting like a madman because we hadn't been met? Well, the man with the Rolls was just coming out of the bar, with a girl trailing behind him. He noticed you, all right." She smiled. "To tell you the truth, I flirted with him, but he only had eyes for you, as the old song goes. So what are you going to do about it?"

"Do? Why—nothing. Nothing at all."

13

Julia fell into a chair among the vases and flowers and shook her pretty head.

"Americans! I don't think I'm ever going to understand you!"

Two

The message to be "ready on time and waiting in the lobby" had been given to both Julia and Lori by the managers from London and Chicago, and so, perfumes mingling, dressed in their best, both girls left the glass elevator promptly at five, Julia looking like British royalty in a pale blue silk that touched the floor, Lori in her cream satin that she had copied from an original. It too was floor length, with a high, empire waist that modestly accentuated her rather full breasts.

The cars to take people to the Consulate cocktail party were lined up in front of the hotel. The lobby was filled with British and American "journalists," as Julia called them, plus some television people sent over to do stories on the beautiful new hotel. It certainly was that, with its gleaming marble floors, luscious thick carpets, and baskets of flowers.

The evening was surprisingly cool. The limos, British and American flags waving from the fronts and sides, crossed the lighted blaze of shops in Rue Fuad and traveled on toward the wide, brightly lighted street that ran alongside the blue Mediterranean. The managers rode with the girls and the talk went to the weather; Lori smiled but finally turned her face to the car window so that she could look at the city.

Alexandria seemed to have raised herself like an old ghost dressed for an evening of mystery and romance. The cars drove slowly; the windows were partway down so that the lemon-scented air drifted in like perfume. On corners, on sidewalks, even in streets, people streamed, walked, speaking fragments of Armenian, Greek, Amharic, Arabic. They were lovely streets, with gleaming white and pink and green houses, wide, spacious lawns, and balconies graced with pots of lush flowers. They drove on, until the lovely well-tended homes were behind them, and now they were passing harbors and ugly streets slippery with discarded fluff from the cotton markets. People stood like ragged children, staring at the big, slow-moving cars that carried the hotel staff toward the Consulate. There were bus stops with strange names like Saba Pacha, Mazloum, Zizinia, Bacos, Schutz, Gianclis—and everywhere there was that odd, fading, mauve-lemon light and the smell of pungent fruit mixed with sea brine.

"Do you have your invitations, ladies?" It was Frank Corita, Lori's boss, his voice nervous and a bit too loud. He was a plump little man, given to harsh breathing and heavy smoking; out of Chicago he felt ill at ease and threatened.

Both Lori and Julia reached into their purses and pulled out the rather large pieces of pasteboard with the printed invitation for cocktails, written in French.

"Good," said Mr. Corita, his heavy face creasing into a smile. "Hang onto them, and since nobody around here speaks French, just keep smiling, so we don't look like we're stupid."

Lori said nothing. Beside her Julia made a small chuckling sound, but she, too, was silent. Thus far the staff had treated the girls kindly but as if they were lowly employees.

The Consulate building was old and covered with a thick, dark-green moss. Lights blazed from it; beyond and to its back was the sea. They were met in the foyer by a small gentleman who spoke in French, and, as they'd been told to do, the girls merely smiled at him.

Then Lori was being led by Frank Corita into another room, beautifully furnished, this one was, with soft lights and people wandering around with drinks in hand, talking. For the next thirty minutes she smiled, nodded, allowed herself to be guided about by Frank, who seemed anxious to tell everyone this was the young lady representing the Hotel Teresa in Chicago. Someone handed her a glass of champagne, one of the men. Frank had drifted off, finally.

". . . in Cannes," one of the men was saying. He was handsome, with silver hair and a slightly dissipated look around his eyes. "Weren't you the actress who got the award for that film . . ."

She had the strangest feeling, as if from somewhere someone was staring at her.

"I'm afraid not. I'm not an actress."

"But your voice! Surely with such a lovely, husky voice—"

"My dear fellow," another man said, "she just told you she isn't in the flicks. Your name is Coleman? Would that be the Palm Beach Colemans?"

"I'm here with the hotel people," Lori said, still feeling as if someone was watching her. She glanced to her left; Julia was talking with a group of people, looking very confident and elegant. She turned back to listen to what was being said, but the feeling seemed stronger than ever now. Someone in the room was staring at her.

She saw him then, finally. He sat at the bar, next to a beautiful, dark-haired girl who wore a backless black dress. He was tall and slender, but his shoulders were wide and muscular-looking in the formal tux. He had very dark eyes and somewhat heavy brows, and he was watching Lori with an intensity that made her face go hot.

Seeing that she met his bold glance, he inclined his head in a formal, brief acknowledgment of their eye encounter, and then, just as she was beginning to be angry because of his staring, he smiled at her.

It was a totally captivating smile, so that for a second in time the two of them seemed to share an unspoken secret, like lovers who suddenly and unexpectedly meet in a strange place after a very long separation.

Lori caught her breath, then turned away as the man at her side touched her arm, asking her another question.

At some point in the polite conversation Lori once again glanced toward the bar; the man with the amused, watchful dark eyes was still looking at her.

This time he winked.

And Lori winked back.

The man at her side was still talking; seconds later Frank Corita was back, guiding her into a larger room where more people had arrived and were wandering around. It was exactly six o'clock by the charming, Louis XIV clock over the room's marble mantel, when Lori finally excused herself and walked up the winding, heavily carpeted staircase to the ladies' powder room. This room, like the others, was skillfully, beautifully decorated, totally French, with exquisite white and gold furniture. Lori sat wearily at the dressing table; her face still felt warm from that stranger's look.

"Do try the perfume. It's *Jamais de la vie,* and men absolutely adore it."

Lori turned around sharply; she had not known anyone

17

else was in the room. It was the girl with the backless dress, lying languidly on one of the couches, her long, lovely legs curled up, her black, short hair falling over her face a bit. She was more stylish than beautiful, and just now her brown eyes were cold as winter coal as she looked at Lori.

"I'm already wearing perfume, thanks," Lori said. She felt vaguely uneasy; this girl had been sitting next to the man who had looked at her in that bold and disturbing way. "You—you're American, aren't you?"

The tanned, bare shoulders shrugged. "I suppose you could say that. I've lived in Monte Carlo and other places for most of my life, though." The tone was cool and somehow snobbish. "You're a cook, a hotel cook or something, aren't you?"

It was such an obvious, nasty insult, that for a second or two Lori could find no suitable answer.

"I work for the hotel, yes."

"As a cook?"

"In the kitchen, yes." Lori met the cold dark eyes. "May I ask why you've decided to hate me? Surely it isn't just because I work in a hotel kitchen."

The girl on the couch swung her long legs to the floor and began putting on chic, thin-heeled shoes. "Of course not. Usually I wouldn't find myself meeting someone like you socially."

Now anger rushed over Lori and her Irish disposition got the best of her.

"I don't know what this is all about, but whatever it is, I'm not going to stand here and listen. Maybe," she said quietly, "you ought to spend more time back home in the States. You'd be surprised to learn how democratic we are there!"

She had gathered up her purse and scarf when the girl's

cold voice stopped her: "He does that sort of thing, you know. Sends flowers and makes a woman feel as if it's fate or something. He's hopelessly addicted to women—they're like a sickness to him. So don't count on anything—permanent."

Lori had turned slowly around. "I haven't the slightest idea," she said, "what you're talking about."

"I'm talking about you and Paul," the girl said evenly, her beautiful eyes smoldering, "and I'm talking about the flowers he sent you, after he did a bit of checking and found out your name."

"Look," Lori told her, "if he's your husband, or . . . or, your boyfriend, I assure you, I haven't—"

"You didn't have to. That's right, it only took one long look at the airport and I knew he was going to go through it all again, this time with a—a silly little cook, for God's sake, from a kitchen in Chicago! And for your information he isn't my husabnd, not yet, but he will be, sooner than he thinks!"

Lori looked at her, at this tall, beautifully dressed girl who was, under her nastiness, obviously very upset.

"Kindly thank your Paul Kardett for the flowers," she said quietly. "And believe me, I'm not interested."

"Is that a promise?"

Lori smiled a wise little smile. "Of course. Any man who would be interested in you couldn't possibly be someone I'd want."

"Listen, I saw you flirting with him at the bar, so don't—"

"Flirting with—" Lori stopped talking. So that was Paul Kardett!

"I mean it," the girl said coldly, "try to make it with Paul and you'll be leaving Alexandria sooner than you'd planned! My father has a lot of power and I—"

19

Lori turned and left the room quickly, closing the door behind her.

"Lori!" It was Julia, coming up to her in the foyer, a glass of pink champagne in her hand. "Here, take this. When I drink, I start talking Cockney. Is something wrong?"

"I think I'll just go on back to the hotel," Lori said a bit unsteadily.

Julia's gray eyes were clouding with worry. "You *are* ill, aren't you?"

"No—it isn't that." Suddenly her eyes misted and she quickly walked toward the front door, not wanting to cry.

"Wait," Julia said, coming up to her, "I'll go with you, but let's not leave our coats here. Wait right here, Luv, and I'll go and fetch the limo. I think they've got them parked in front."

And so a few minutes later both girls climbed inside the big car once again and through the new rain and darkness were driven across town, back to the Hotel Teresa.

Lori was in the bathroom. For some unexplainable reason she had taken off her clothes and now, huddled in her robe, she stood with her back against the closed and locked door.

"Are you being sick in there or something?" Julia's voice was concerned and a bit motherly. Worry or emotion seemed to change her upper-class British accent into a slight Cockney.

Lori took a deep breath. "No," she said, moving away from the door, unlocking it. "I'm fine now." She faced Julia. "Honestly."

"You are absolutely not at all fine," Julia said sternly. "What the devil happened at the Consulate?"

"Julia," Lori said carefully, "you're being very good to me, but I'd rather not talk about it if you don't mind."

Julia surveyed her steadily. "Let's see. You went to the powder room; before that you were fine. As a matter of fact I heard from someone that Paul Kardett was very interested in you, and that's why he sent all these flowers. And speaking of flowers what happened to most of them?" Only two small vases remained, pale cream-colored roses. The rest, all the baskets and containers that had filled the room near to brimming, had disappeared.

Lori shrugged, settling herself by the glass patio doors that opened onto the balcony. The view calmed her, seemed to put things in proper perspective. This city had been here for thousands of years. Her own anger at the cruel words of a stupid woman began to seem foolish and insignificant.

"I had them sent to the kitchen," she told Julia. "I thought the cooks and bakers might like them. You don't mind, do you?"

"Of course I don't mind. But you've missed the point, Lori, and that is that a very handsome and sought-after man is definitely after you!"

"After me? I don't think I like the sound of that." She leaned back in the chair, watching the rain.

The phone rang, startling both of them. Julia answered it, spoke softly, then hung up. For a brief moment she seemed to be busy looking through her closet. Lori was silent, letting the rage flow out of her. That woman in the backless dress, whoever she was, had introduced snobbery and prejudice into Lori's life. Until tonight she had never experienced it.

Julia was at the phone again. "—with milk, please," she said into the phone. Then she turned to Lori, her face

21

somehow masked. "You had a call a moment ago, but we'll talk about that after tea. Tea is very good for the soul, did you know that? A few years back a German girl won the popularity contest at the Teresa Hotel in Frankfort. Her prize was to go to London, where she was treated about the same as you and I are treated here: parties and staff meetings and the big constant smile—you know what I mean. Anyway she was drinking her tea out of a glass, the way they do in Germany, when a man at the next table noticed her, and within two weeks he'd married her. Now she has a house in Stratford and a summer place at Dover, and—are you listening, Lori?"

"Did you say I had a phone call?"

"This," Julia said, ignoring the question, "is none other than my strawberry mask. Now hold still; I'll just put a bit here, and here, and this plus the tea will have you fit as a fiddle in plenty of time to borrow my best dress and go."

Lori sat up straighter, submitting to the dabs of strawberry-scented cream on her face.

"Go? Go where? Julia, I've got a feeling that you're up to something!"

"Not at all, Luv. Now kindly hold still while I put some on your nose. It doesn't take away freckles, but American girls don't mind them the way we do, do you?"

"Julia, would you mind telling me who phoned me?"

Julia, who had been leaning over Lori, fawning over her like a mother hen, suddenly sat on the floor cross-legged.

"I just figured it out," she said. "I think I know what happened, and it happened in the powder room, didn't it?"

"I told you," Lori said, "I want to forget that. Would you please—"

"That she-devil! I saw her ogling you, watching you like some kind of killer bird, so jealous you could practically see steam coming out of her ears! So she went up there and

22

waited for you to come up and when you did, she—what did she say to you?"

"Nothing important. It's past now, and I want to forget it. Look," Lori said earnestly, "I'm not going to let anything or anybody spoil this trip for me! You see, I need time, time to be away from home, time to . . . to think about Tom in a different way."

"Time to fall in love with someone else, that's what you need," Julia said. "Which brings us to your call."

"Do you think Mr. Corita will fire me if I tell him I don't want to go back to the Consulate party tonight?"

"The call," Julia said, "wasn't from your boss." Her eyes were shining. "It was Paul Kardett, and he wants you to meet him downstairs in an hour. He has something important to tell you, he said."

Lori got quickly up from the chair. "I'm sorry, but—"

"Think about it a moment. You came here to forget, didn't you?"

Lori hesitated a second. "Yes," she admitted finally, "I suppose I did."

"Well, he can help you do that, you know."

Lori shook her head. "You don't understand. He—that man is some kind of professional womanizer! He must have hundreds of girls panting after him, and I'm not about to be taken in by the fact that he'd like to add another American to his list!"

Julia said nothing. She had taken down one of her dresses from the closet, and now she was holding it up to Lori, her eyes narrowed.

"Fits fine," she said. "It'll take a bit of tucking here, but other than that, its going to fit like skin. We'll have tea and then I'll help you with your hair."

"Julia, I told you—"

Julia smiled wisely. "I know. But we'll have tea and maybe you'll change your mind, after all."

Lori did change her mind, but not because of the heavily honeyed tea or even because of the unexpected, single, breathtakingly beautiful gardenia that was sent to her moments later, along with a brief note from Paul, asking her to join him in the East Room for dinner. Even Julia's dress, a gold lamé which looked straight out of the twenties, didn't really convince her.

Instead it was the exciting, tingling thought of being alone with that handsome, mysterious man, if only for one evening—that did it.

Three

Rain fell in sheets outside as Lori walked from the glass elevator through the nearly deserted lobby. The cocktail hour was over; most of the hotel's guests were either in one of the crowded dining rooms or had gone looking for some excitement outside the hotel.

She felt vastly uncomfortable in the short dress; the material was soft enough next to her skin, for the dress was lined, but the glittering metallic fabric kept catching at her purse and the dress was, to Lori's way of thinking, outrageously sensual, far too much so. But Julia had insisted, saying the gold caught the gold in Lori's brown hair and in her greenish eyes.

Paul Kardett was nowhere to be seen. Outside the big limos were at the curb, the drivers dozing inside them.

"Ms. Coleman?" It was the hotel's new manager, a polite, smiling Egyptian who had been at the cocktail party earlier. He took Lori's arm. "Right this way," he told her. "Supper will be served shortly."

She was not hungry, but a sudden mental picture of her boss, telling her to smile, came unexpectedly into her mind and she nodded almost without thinking. They crossed the quiet lobby and the manager tapped at a door.

It was opened by Paul Kardett.

Face to face with him this way, she felt her heart quicken; he was even better looking than she had at first thought. His skin was a golden color, smooth and clear, and his features were masculine and yet almost beautiful. She saw that he had long, thick lashes that any woman would envy, and that his dark eyes were very serious as he bowed briefly, his lips touching the top of her hand.

"I've arranged for some steaks to be sent in," he told her. "Beef isn't easy to get here, but I understand Americans like it." He smiled, and in that single smile she saw why women were so attracted to him. "Would you like a glass of wine?"

She walked into the room; it was large, ornate, done in velvets and dark colors, with a fire in the fireplace. She suddenly wondered if perhaps she hadn't made a mistake by coming. This man would be easy to fall in love with— and she was beginning to understand that she had been seeking a love affair, the right love affair, for some time, in order to blot out the grief that seemed never to go completely away.

"No thank you." She was acutely uncomfortable of the fact that he was once again looking at her, not rudely, but openly, as if the sight of her pleased him.

"Very well, then," he said, "sit down for a moment, little Yank; I want to talk to you."

The name he had given her made her feel somehow

more at ease. She chose a brown velvet chair and her body sank into it.

"Thank you for the flowers, Mr. Kardett."

His English was nearly perfect, with just a trace of British in it.

"Paul. Look, I know what happened to you this evening and I want to apologize for her. I'm really terribly sorry." His dark eyes were serious. "Francine seems to think she owns the world."

"Even if she did, she wouldn't own the people in it. Anyway I'm not going to think about it anymore."

"Good. Now have a little wine." He poured from a small decanter and raised his glass. "To your stay in Alexandria. May it be whatever you want it to be." He took a sip, holding the glass in two hands, watching her again.

The room was beginning to seem much less cold, or maybe it was that being even this close to this man warmed her. Was that possible?

"Do you always do her apologizing for her?" She hadn't meant to mention the incident and yet something had driven her to. The truth was she found herself wondering just what the relationship between them really was.

He laughed. "Certainly not. Francine's sins are far too many for me to go around trying to right things. But someone told me they saw you come out of the powder room looking pale and upset, and since I know that tongue of hers—"

"Let's forget it then, shall we?"

His eyes deepened. "Good. Are you getting hungry?"

"I'm afraid not. And I really can't stay long, I just wanted to thank you for the flowers and for making me feel so welcome here."

"Please don't run off so soon," he said quickly, getting out of his chair. "We can eat later, then. I thought you

26

might be getting tired of curry sauce and stuffed birds, but somehow, I think you like Alexandria. I think you . . . feel at ease here. Do you?"

She met his dark eyes. "Yes. I don't understand it, but for some reason, I feel—"

"That you've been here before?"

She let her breath out. "Yes, that's it exactly! I wasn't sure before, but I believe that's it." She shook her head. "What I mean is, that's what it seems to be, but of course it isn't really."

He poured more wine into her nearly full glass. "It's called Karma," he said quietly. "And you might as well know that from the very first instant I saw you, I felt—something. That you were different from the usual American tourist. I felt that you somehow . . . belonged in this city."

She could feel the excitement beginning in her, the sense of closeness to this man, of intimacy, even though they sat apart and no part of them was touching. No physical part.

"Do you want to have a look at Alexandria, Ms. Coleman? She can be many things to many people."

She smiled into his eyes. "She?"

"Of course. The most beautiful of life is female, so naturally, Alexandria is, too."

Lori suddenly remembered that this man was purported to be "addicted" to women. She must be careful not to take him seriously.

His car was a Renault, small and extremely comfortable. They drove in the rain, past the Municipal Gardens, where he stopped to point out the iron grilles, gleaming with wetness. Then they passed a street called Tatwig and the headlights began to pick out anthill cafés crowded with people. He parked in a dark, narrow street near the mosque, then opened the car door for her, taking her hand. Once again she felt that strange jolt of excitement course through her at his touch. Together they hurried through the rain, past tenement houses with dismal shutters and peeling paint.

"Are you all right?"

"Of course; why shouldn't I be?" The chilly rain felt good on her hot face.

"Then get your courage up," he said, smiling charmingly at her, "because just around the corner is a very terrible café where nobody will bother us. You see, I want to be alone with you." He sounded teasing, and yet, some deep look of seriousness had come into those dark eyes.

Still holding hands, they crossed the street and rounded the corner. He pulled her into a darkish doorway, his body shielding her's from the downpour.

"There's no menu, but you'll be pleasantly surprised, I think, at the food and wine."

She realized she was actually hungry, that the cruel words of the girl named Francine seemed to have made her somehow determined, but she didn't know in just what way. At any rate she was here with this stranger, in a city that, until very recently, had only been a vague name to her. This was a different world, a world of dark streets, oddly shaped buildings, a brilliantly blue sea, and secrets.

The Café Pompey was tucked into the street like an afterthought. It was filled with people; they sat at every table, stood three deep at the long bar, spoke in what seemed to be at least ten languages. The large room was shadowy, lit only by the feeble light of rushlights. This peculiar light, pushing up from the mud floor, touched faces and cheekbones and chattering mouths, giving everyone an unreal, surrealistic look, like actors made up for a play.

An Arab waiter saw Paul at once and came up to him, speaking softly in French. Paul nodded and, still holding tightly to Lori's hand, led her to a small table in a dark corner with a *Reserved* sign on it, printed in French, Arabic, and English. A bottle of chilled wine waited for them; there was a thick candle on the table near a basket of chunky black bread.

Lori settled herself at the table, tasting the wine Paul poured for her. She felt relaxed, and slowly her body warmed itself from the rain.

"You are in one of the oldest cafés in the city," Paul told her. "I thought you would prefer a place like this to . . . your American hotel dining room."

"Yes," she said quietly, and without another word he reached across the table and covered her hand with his. And so, for a while, until the thick soup came, they sat that way, in comfortable silence, touching, drinking the deep red wine. Lori realized suddenly, when he let go her hand, that all the pain, the sorrow and longing, and the discontent that she had felt since that horrible night when she learned of Tommy's death, all that was gone, disappeared like smoke in the wind. It wasn't that she had forgotten the young man she had once loved; it was only that her grief seemed to have left. In the crooked streets, in this dim café, with this stranger, she felt whole again.

The soup was delicious, rich with lamb and curry and fresh vegetables. Outside the open window, odors—too many to count—rose to meet them: tar, fish, lemon-rain mixed with carnations. A flower seller began her chant:

"Carnations, sweet, sweet, sweet as the breath of your lover. . . ."

Paul's eyes met hers over the candlelight.

"Would you like a flower?"

He didn't wait for her answer; he got up and hurried outside. Lori felt high, dizzy from it all, as if she were dreaming some lovely, special dream. For a moment she tried to think of home, Chicago, the look of the streets in the morning, the bus she took to work, the huge kitchen at the hotel, and her corner of it, the sights and sounds and smells of her work and her life there.

But those things were lost to her, gone from her mind for now, anyway. Instead she found that she wanted to be no place else in the world but here, here in this busy place with the delicious food and the mud floor and the thick black bread—and a man totally different from anyone she had ever known before.

He came back with his arms filled with carnations, red and pink and white, sweet-smelling, nearly overpowering. Some of them fell on the mud floor; the little table was covered with them.

"You have too many."

"No," he said quietly, looking at her face. "You make me want to . . . to buy you things, to do things for you. I cannot tell you the pleasure I feel when I see you smile."

Stop, she thought, stop making me feel so good, so happy! Because if what Francine had said were true, then Paul did this with all the women he wanted, lavished gifts on them, made them feel as if they were beautiful and special and deeply desirable.

A pretty, dark-skinned woman was singing a song up on the tiny stage. Her voice was husky and beautiful; it didn't matter to Lori that she couldn't understand the words. It was a love song, haunting and sad.

"Are you crying?" Paul gently touched her face with one finger. "Tears," he said quietly. "Why?"

She shook her head.

"I know what you need," he said suddenly, "you need to go somewhere with me where there is laughter and dancing and good times and joy. And I know just such a place. You do like weddings, don't you?"

"Weddings?"

"Yes, a friend of mine invited me to the marriage of his sister. I hadn't planned to go, but now, I think it would be a very good idea."

She smiled. "Don't you like weddings, Paul?"

For an instant his eyes clouded. It was as if some invisible curtain had been drawn; he was no longer ardent and attentive and admiring. He seemed to have withdrawn from her, to have gone into some secret place of his own mind and heart.

"Sometimes," he said finally. "This one, yes, I'm sure I'll like this one. Shall we go?"

The waiter brought him a slip of paper; no money exchanged hands. Outside they once again hurried through the slick rain to his car, but this time, inside, instead of starting the car immediately, he turned to her, his tanned face grave.

"Do you mind if I kiss you?"

She felt her breath catch. A kiss, what possible harm could there be in a single kiss?

For answer she raised her face, closing her eyes. She felt his lips, warm and searching, close over hers. His arms held her; she felt lost in the strength of them, in the nearness of his body. His mouth was her refuge; instead of pulling away rather quickly she felt her own arms go around his neck, holding him, pulling him to her. Her mouth answered his question, that unspoken question that begged for touching, for ecstasy . . .

Then it was over. He had thrust her from him, turned and started the car very quickly, so that the tires made a squealing sound on the wet pavement. In the light from the dashboard his handsome face looked almost ashen.

"Paul, what is it?"

"I knew it," he said almost to himself, "I sensed it." He looked at her briefly, his eyes smoldering. "From the first

31

second I saw you at the airport, I sensed it. You have the power," he said, and he turned back to his driving.

"I have *what*?"

"Kismet," he said softly. "Destiny. I doubt if either of us can do anything about it."

"Look, I haven't the slightest idea what you're talking about." But in fact she did, to some degree. From the onset there had been a very powerful magnetism between them, some force at work, drawing them together, and when they were together, some terrible need seemed to be eased, at least for Lori.

Was it possible that this man, with his obvious wealth and influence and all the women in his life, still felt that need, still lacked something in his life?

She closed her eyes, giving herself up to the cozy warmth of the car, the heavy aroma of the carnations on the seat beside her, the feeling of the good food and wine inside her, the nearness and protection of Paul. When she opened them, they were driving along the sea and the rain had slacked somewhat.

The house where the wedding was faced the sea; it was very lovely with servants' quarters in a small separate building. From there a child cried steadily and a woman crooned to it. At the big house lights blazed and the happy sound of raised voices and loud music floated out to them.

"Paul, do you mind if I give the bride the carnations?"

"Of course not," he told her. "I'd planned to send something around in the morning, a gift, but for now, the flowers will do nicely. I'll buy you more tomorrow."

"I don't want you buying me things."

"That's part of what bothers me," he told her, parking the car near the sea wall. "You aren't going to let me do it all my way, are you?"

"I don't want—"

He silenced her by kissing her again. This time he pulled her to him roughly, as soon as she stepped outside the car. The wind from the dark sea blew the hair at the front of her face, and as he held her, Paul reached into her hair and took the pins from it, touching her soft hair until he found each one, until at last it was free and tumbled down around her bare shoulders. His mouth left hers briefly, brushing her throat hungrily as his hands, warm and yearning, cupped her breasts.

"Paul!" It was a young man in a low sports car; his headlights nearly blinded them in the glare. "Good to see you here, old chap. I didn't think you went to weddings."

"I don't, usually. Will you turn your dammed lights off, Dobbie?"

"Oh," the British voice said, "Sorry, old man." He parked the car and strode toward them, a dapper young man, well dressed and smiling, extending his hand in greeting. "I see you've captivated the most beautiful girl in Alexandria," he said, smiling warmly at Lori. "An American—now that's very interesting."

"Stay away from Dobbie," Paul said lightly. "He lives off his grandfather's fortune and spends most of his time drinking and trying to end it all in fast boats. Oh—and he loves weddings, having had four or maybe five of them himself."

"Four and a half," Dobbie said, laughing good-naturedly. "The last one ended in annulment. Come along, little girl, take my arm and I'll show you how to dance the wedding dance in Alexandria!"

It was impossible not to like that brash young man with the thin face and intelligent blue eyes. In spite of Paul's teasing Lori felt that the two men, Paul and Dobbie, were close friends. So, inside the lovely house, after presenting the rain-wet carnations to the bride, Lori danced the wedding dance with Dobbie, to the sound of the Eastern music with

33

its strange, beautiful instruments, heavy sensual beat, and tinkling bells.

When the dance was finished, there was a flurry of introductions; everyone seemed pleased to have Paul there. There were long tables filled with delicious-looking food, and although she wasn't hungry, Lori accepted a plate and nibbled at the spiced chicken and figs and nuts, so as not to offend her hostess.

Men—old, young, smiling, somber—all wanted to dance with her. The wine she'd had with Paul at the café made her feel light as a feather, and after a while, she wasn't at all sure whom she danced with; she only knew that she was enjoying herself, basking in the warm feeling of joy that filled that home. How lovely, she thought. How beautiful to be married and young and lovely, and to have all your guests so happy for you! The thought of Tommy began to surface in her mind, but in that instant Paul cut in and she was dancing her first dance with him. He must have waited for this dance; the lights had been dimmed and only candles were lit, so that the room glowed softly in a spreading, golden hue. The music was low, sensual, quiet now, and she leaned her head on his shoulder, giving herself to the rhythm and pulse of the music. He was an expert dancer, holding her lightly but closely, his hand on the small of her back, touching her bare skin, for the borrowed dress was nearly backless. Once he slid his hand upward, so that it tangled itself in her long hair, and she felt herself trembling.

The music stopped and Paul led her to a corner, where velvet cushions had been spread on the floor. There he pulled her down beside him, so that they sat closely, watching as an Arab boy placed two straight-backed chairs in the center of the now-empty floor. The dancing had stopped; there was an air of hushed waiting in the room. More candles were lit by the boy; the room gleamed in their pale, flickering light. Then the young bride and her husband came to the center of the room and, not looking at each other, sat on the chairs.

The bride's pretty face was impassive as the music began, low at first, then it became a throbbing beat, sensual and fast. Lori expected the young married couple to dance; she thought that was what would happen next, but they made no sign of moving from their chairs or even glancing at each other.

Then from the shadows a young woman suddenly appeared. She was barefoot and she wore the traditional dress of the belly dancer: a brief top and a long, sheer skirt that exposed her legs when she moved, a wide satin band around her moving hips. She began to dance with her arms above her head; she carried a tambourine and from time to time she shook it. Her long black hair was down her back and her ankle and wrist bracelets made little clinking sounds. She was very pretty and quite an extraordinary dancer.

As the dance progressed, the girl moved closer to the groom; finally she stood directly in front of him, dancing only for him, her hip movements very suggestive, her body swaying, long hair partly over her face. From time to time, it seemed to Lori, she turned her attention from the impassive groom and glanced toward where Paul sat next to Lori, on the cushioned floor.

The music became wild and very loud, the dancer threw out her arms and tossed back her hair, her eyes closed. She raised her arms as the climax to the music came, then she opened them, staring boldly and directly at Paul!

Then she quickly left the room, going through a door in the shadows.

There was much clapping and movement; people got to their feet, began drinking more wine; the music began again, soft and happy. The bride and groom shook hands and looked as if that odd, sensual dance had not taken place, or if it had, they seemed not to be concerned or embarrassed by it.

"Perhaps," Paul said beside Lori, "I should explain the meaning of the Love Dance to you. It's part of the marriage ritual, you see. The groom must not show lust for his virgin bride, so to . . . prepare him . . . a dancing girl is brought in for that purpose. I hope you weren't uncomfortable."

Lori realized she was embarrassed somewhat, but there were so many Eastern customs she didn't know about and wanted to, that she was determined not to let Paul know her true reaction.

"The bride is lovely," she said, changing the subject. "She was very sweet about the flowers, Paul."

He looked down at her. "I like the way you say my name," he told her, his voice low. "The rain stopped. Would you like to go to my island and have an early breakfast?"

"Do you mean stay all night with you?"

He smiled. "Well, I suppose you could put it that way. I've never thought of my island as being enchanted, but if you come there, I'm sure it will be. Please," he said quietly, "and I promise you a view of the sea you won't find anywhere else in the world!"

People, guests, were beginning to leave, bowing, the men embracing and kissing in the Eastern fashion. Lori reached for her purse and scarf.

"Do you mean you have an island all your own?"

"Yes; it's mine now, since my father died. I don't stay

there too much, its a lonely place at best. You'll come with me?"

"No," she said quickly, "I couldn't. I mean—I'm due at a morning staff meeting and it wouldn't do for me to be late because I'm at some remote island getting a good look at the sea!" She purposely made her voice light and joking. "I think I should be getting back to the hotel now, if you don't mind."

"I do mind, of course, but whatever you wish." He was, she knew, clearly disappointed, but once again Francine's ugly warning came into her mind. If women were an addiction to this man, Lori knew she would only be one of many girls he had fancied himself to be in love with at one time or another.

And what about Francine? What, Lori wondered, was that beautiful, nasty female doing while Paul was squiring Lori around town?

"May I see you tomorrow, Lori?"

Her thoughts of Francine made her hesitate. "I'm not sure," she said, her voice careful. "What I mean is, there might be meetings all day, for all I know."

"May I phone you, then?"

"Yes, of course."

"Lori," he said, "is something wrong? I thought, before, it seemed to me that together, we were nearly perfect. But now—"

"It's nothing," she told him, not meeting his worried eyes. "I just think I'd better get back to the hotel."

But they both knew that the moments of closeness had left them, and that now, instead of feeling like happy friends or lovers-to-be they were somehow overly eager to find Dobbie and to listen to his slightly drunk chatter and gossip.

They said good night finally, to their host and hostess,

then began the walk down the beach to the Renault. As they left the house a figure suddenly appeared on the sand, standing alone in the dim moonlight. Lori stopped walking, startled.

"Isn't that—isn't someone there motioning to you, Paul?"

Indeed she was, and as the clouds passed over the pale moon Lori saw that the figure on the beach was the dancing girl, wearing some sort of cloak over her costume. She was barefoot, standing alone on the quiet beach, her hair blowing in the night wind. Somehow the sight of her, her white arms beckoning, was disturbing.

"Paul, she's trying to get your attention! Shouldn't you—"

"It's only Jasmine," he said. "She's a little crazy sometimes. Come on, let's get out of here."

He started the car. The headlights suddenly brought into brilliant clarity the figure on the beach; Lori got a brief glimpse of the lovely and somehow angry-looking young face as Paul's car sped away. She leaned back in the seat, feeling her hands begin to tremble slightly, there in her lap.

"Perhaps she had something important to say to you."

"Jasmine? There is nothing important in her life. There could be, but she chooses to have it not so. Instead she worries about me and my life."

A thousand or more questions rose in Lori's mind about the girl. Obviously Paul knew her, perhaps knew her very well. They might, she thought with a sudden feeling of fleeting pain, be lovers. Well, what if they were; it was nothing to her. She hardly knew Paul Kardett, except to have heard that he cared more for women than was good for him.

They rode the rest of the way in silence, not the comfortable silence they'd had earlier, when his warm hand had been over hers, when she'd felt his pulse beating in his clasp, but a chilly silence that ended only when he pulled up in front of the big hotel, parking just behind the limos.

"Good night," she said quickly. "Thank you for a very memorable night."

"That sounds like good-bye. Is it?"

Something, a fullness, rose in her throat. She felt a fool to be so emotionally involved at such an early time in a relationship, but for some reason she couldn't seem to help herself.

"I—I don't know. I'm not sure whether or not it should be good-bye."

He looked steadily into her eyes for a heartbeat or two, then, with a kind of moaning sound, he pulled her into his arms and kissed her once again. This time Lori struggled, but only briefly. The wonder and warmth and absolute feeling of something very close to total joy filled her, so much so that she gave herself up to the feelings, those wild, unleashed feelings she had thought died with the boy she had once loved.

"Lori—Lori—" his voice was muffled, thick with emotion. He cupped her face between his strong hands, bending to kiss her yet another time.

She forced herself to draw away from him, to remember who she was and where she came from and where she was now, in a place so far from home, so totally different from home, from her life there. And once again Francine's ugly warning flashed into her mind.

"Good night," she said. "Paul, please, let me go."

He released her without a word, got out of his car, and opened the car door for her. She hurried past him into the deserted hotel lobby, hoping nobody would see her flushed face and feverish-looking eyes.

* * *

Julia was asleep, thank goodness, when Lori let herself in the bedroom, using her key. She got out of the borrowed dress, hung it up, brushed her teeth, avoided looking at her reflection because she knew how she must look—like a woman who has nearly been made love to and perhaps wishes she had been.

But she did not get into her bed. It was a lovely time, this time before the cool, soft morning began, and she wanted to watch the city rouse itself, feel its charm and power, with its flat landscape and exhausted airs.

She sat on the balcony until morning came at last, an early spring dawn with its dense dew, just before the birds began their song. As she got up to go inside, a high sweet voice came from the nearby mosque, a singsong voice that hung on the palm-cooled air like a poised lark, high and sweet:

I praise the perfection of God, the Forever existing,
The perfection of God the Desired, the Existing,
The Single, the Supreme, the perfection of God,
The one, the Sole, the perfection of Him
Who taketh unto Himself no male or female partner,
Nor any like Him, nor any that is disobedient—
His perfection be extolled.

The ancient, great prayer wound its way into her mind until the whole morning seemed bathed with its marvelous healing powers. Balcony doors across the street began to open; women came out sleepily, some with babies on their hips. The pungent aroma of spiced coffee mixed with lemon air and flowers filled her senses.

She went to bed and lay with her face to the windows. Somewhere in the city, or perhaps out on his island, slept a man who had, in a very short space of time, taken possession of her very soul.

Four

The girls were awakened the next morning by a discreet tapping at their bedroom door. It was Julia who woke first, raising herself up on one smooth elbow to call out in a somewhat thick voice, asking who it was.

"It is Mickey Mouse, if you please, with a message for you ladies: the staff meeting will begin in thirty minutes. I have put coffee outside your door. Thank you very much."

This time, Lori sat up, staring at the closed door.

"Did he say his name was Mickey Mouse?"

"Just a little joke, Luvvie. Some of the newspaper people turned him on to Mickey, along with a Mouseketeer hat." Julia got out of bed and headed for the door. She was wearing an extremely ugly nightgown that she had told Lori, was very dear to her because she could wrap her toes in it while sleeping. She carried the tray inside the room. "He brings coffee, no more tea. Although I must admit it smells delicious." She began pouring. "Isn't there an embassy party this evening?"

"I heard they're coming here, for cocktails, instead. But it isn't obligatory that we go, thank goodness. That should give us time to shop."

Julia sipped her coffee thoughtfully. "And what about your evening? Was my dress an absolute smash?"

"Absolutely." Lori felt her face flush a bit. "We went to a wedding."

"A wedding! Maybe that," Julia said, beginning to pull back the draperies at the window, "is part of his method."

41

Suddenly Lori regretted having mentioned her date with Paul. It was clear that Julia had a lot of questions to ask.

"Well, tell me about it! What'd he say—did he spend a lot of money on you?"

Lori headed for the bathroom as a means of escape. "I have no idea about prices in this country. Excuse me, I want to wash my hair before that staff meeting."

But Julia's voice followed her, even through the closed bathroom door.

"I get the feeling you're avoiding me."

Lori turned off the steamy shower water. "What?"

"I said I found out some very interesting facts about your Paul Kardett."

Lori turned on the water once again. "He isn't 'my' Paul Kardett. And I'm not interested in gossip so early in the morning."

"How about over lunch then?" Julia's voice was raised over the shower water. "Stop pretending you aren't interested!"

She was, of course she was, and it became increasingly difficult not to question Julia about her "facts" as the morning wore on. As she'd dressed, putting on a morning-blue cotton dress that suited her hair, with its bright, gold highlights, Lori had felt certain Paul would call her this morning. She even thought she could imagine the sound of his voice, deep yet quiet, speaking to her on the phone, asking her to spend the rest of the day with him.

But she was wrong; he didn't call. The meeting began, in that large, airy room just off the lobby, at precisely eight-thirty. The air conditioner had not yet been turned on; the long windows were open to street sounds and the salty sea air. Everybody sat around the polished table trying not to look sleepy, including Julia, who seemed to be having a lot of difficulty not letting her yawn out.

Twice a bellboy came in with messages, but neither time were they for Lori. She tried harder to concentrate on what the manager of the Hotel Teresa here in Alexandria was saying. He was a stocky, handsome man with silver hair who dressed in Western fashion and spoke with hardly a trace of an accent as he told them of the wonders of the new hotel. It rivaled, he said, the palaces of the Roman Empire, with some of the rooms featuring small dining rooms where hotel guests could recline as they feasted on delicious gourmet food.

Lori gazed out the window at the street beyond, where people filed up and down like characters passing across a stage. She found herself wondering how many of them were happy and satisfied, how many of them went about the daily business of living with light hearts. That one—the lovely woman with the sheer, black veil over part of her face—did her man love her? At night, in his arms, could she shut out the world, forget the worries she'd burdened herself with all day and feel cherished and safe?

"—in progress, although of course, our lucky winners here, these two beautiful young ladies, cannot enter our Hotel Teresa's Most Popular Employee Contest a second time, unfortunately. We at the Teresas like to play fair and square, giving everybody, right down to the youngest busboy, a chance to travel. We like to show the world that we're the best darned hotel chain on the face of this globe!"

Frank Corita paused, waiting for the applause that followed, although it was more polite than enthusiastic. Lori felt herself being nudged by Julia, and she forced herself to listen more attentively and not let her mind wander that way. Frank was sitting down, wiping his round face with a fancy handkerchief. Now Mr. Mulvaney himself was going to make a speech; his pinkish face beamed at them as he put down his coffee cup, adjusted his vest, glanced at his pocket watch and, looking more like Santa Claus then ever, began to tell them about his humble beginnings back in Chicago.

The door opened to the room; a silent Arab boy closed it and walked to the far wall, where he stood, eyes staring at the ceiling, hands behind his back. Mr. Mulvaney droned on; he had reached the part of his story where he told of his first hotel job, at a fleabag place which was now the site of the world-famous Chicago Hotel Teresa. Lori found herself looking at the boy who stood against the wall, his young face impassive. Did he have a message? Or was he there to perhaps see who had an empty coffee cup?

He opened his eyes and looked first at Julia, then at Lori. Lori felt her heart quicken, but it was the more aggressive Julia who got up, sliding her armchair silently over the thick plush rug, and walking quickly to the boy, whispering to him, nodding, took a note from him.

"It's for you," she told Lori, her voice a whisper. She sat down smoothly, sliding the note, which was written on thick white paper that resembled some kind of linen, into Lori's hand. "Do you still want to hear what I found out about him?"

The small, folded, and sealed paper lay in the palm of Lori's hand. Soft as satin, that paper was, proper and somehow formal, and yet, even the feeling of a note, a message from him, had somehow altered her feelings about her life in that moment. She looked out the window again and saw not only the people who walked by, but the city in which they lived. By midmorning, which it now was, the city was fully awake, like a dispairing woman who gets up and begins at once to powder her face. The sun had come out and the splashes of grass in front of shops and on the sloping hills outside the city glistened like fragile green glass. The world looked beautiful to Lori, and if she asked herself why, she didn't let the surprising answer frighten her.

The meeting finally ended; they all shook hands and began to file out. One of the vice-presidents was in the process of asking Lori to have lunch when Julia came up from behind and grabbed Lori's hand.

"We have to hurry," she said, "excuse us, please."

There wasn't time to say a word. Lori allowed herself to be more or less guided out of the hotel, onto the throbbing street, and into the canopied entrance of some sort of coffee shop where hot sweets were also sold. The place had a heady air about it; two men wearing turbans stared boldly as Julia and Lori sat down at one of the tables in the shade.

"Well," Julia said practically, "aren't you going to open it?"

"Of course." She realized she would have liked to be alone to read it. "But not just now, if you don't mind."

"But—whyever not?"

Lori took a small breath. "I'm not sure. To tell you the truth, I guess that man frightens me a little."

Julia leaned back in the chair, ignoring the stares of the grinning men.

"Women seem to turn men on around here without even trying. I'm not sure," she said, beginning to smile, "if I really mind that so much, however!"

"Julia, maybe we should have let Mr. What's-his-name take us to lunch. I don't think he was very happy when we left him standing in the lobby that way."

Julia closed her pretty eyes. "I'm so sick of being nice to people when I don't feel like it! I got this job by smiling and looking pretty and being pleasant, and I won the contest by smiling and looking pretty and being pleasant." She

45

sighed. "I'd love to be myself for a while, but I seldom get the chance!"

Lori smiled. "Go ahead—you're safe with me. I promise not to tell anybody that you really don't smile twenty-four hours a day."

They settled into a small, comfortable silence, while the waiter brought luscious, chilled fruit in a wooden bowl. It was just cool enough to be almost perfect as Lori cut into the rich honeydew melon. Across from her Julia was systematically peeling a very large orange.

"I'll probably get a fashion model's job after all's said and done," Julia said finally. "It's a cinch, now that I've been here. I'm having some pictures taken here, by the way, near the sea. Then I'll take my packet of photographs and start hounding all the model agencies in London."

"I'll probably see you on all the right covers," Lori said.

"Oh, you needn't smile; I'm quite serious. I've always wanted to lead the good life, as I told you, and modeling will get me there a lot faster than working behind the front desk at a hotel will. Unless, of course, I get lucky, the way you seem to have."

"I don't know what you mean." It wasn't that she didn't like Julia, because she did. It was only that some of the girl's ideas seemed all wrong, twisted around.

"But not," Julia said evenly, "as lucky as you might think." She surveyed Lori with calm eyes. "Your new friend has quite a reputation, you know. And I think you ought to know why."

Lori let her breath out, certain that Julia wanted to be helpful but not at all sure she wanted to hear anything bad about Paul Kardett. Somehow it seemed disloyal, to be sitting here ready to bend her head and listen to stories about him.

"I don't think I care why," she told Julia. "I went out

46

with him last night; that's all. That's no reason for me to want some sort of personal inventory taken of his life-style!" She realized that she wasn't being totally honest, that she was extremely curious about whatever it was that Julia knew. It just didn't, however, seem right for her to listen. Not with his note tucked in one corner of her straw purse, next to her rosary, which her mother had dropped into her purse at the airport.

"You mean it doesn't matter to you that he'll never be the groom at any of those beautiful weddings they have around here?"

"Why," Lori asked, "should that matter?"

Julia shrugged. "I just feel that a girl should know what her chances for marriage are when she goes out with a man, even if she only dates him a few times. And your chances with this man are practically nil."

Lori put down her fork. "Why are you telling me this?"

"Because I like you, of course. And if you're seriously looking for a husband—"

"I'm not."

"Or if you're seriously looking for a lover—"

"I'm not."

The skillfully made-up eyes widened. "Well, then, what *do* you want from a man?"

"Nothing," Lori said quietly. "Absolutely nothing."

"That's very hard to believe, Duckie. Look, if you weren't interested in bettering yourself in one way or another, why'd you enter the contest?"

"I didn't," Lori said, smiling. "The head baker put my name in, that's all. Nobody really thought I'd win."

"You're very pretty, why shouldn't you win?"

Lori shrugged. "Maybe I don't . . . get carried away with the idea of being superloyal to the hotel."

"Look, why don't we take a walk and perhaps we'll both

47

feel better about things? I promise not to tell you nasty things about Paul Kardett. Agreed?"

"Agreed," Lori said, smiling.

And so, as the sun grew higher and the day grew hotter, they walked through the old streets, shopping, not spending much money but having a lovely time. Sometimes a sea-washed breeze would waft through, along with the mingled aroma of cooking and spiced food, and Lori thought it the most delightful place she had ever been.

They got back to the hotel before teatime, barely avoiding having to join several hotel people in the lobby for a drink. They escaped by pleading jet lag, although Julia said that that one was getting a bit stale.

"There's supposed to be a prince staying in the hotel," Julia said, trying on the dangling earrings she'd bought at one of the stands. "He's from one of those tiny countries where everybody is superrich. Would you like to go hunting with me?"

Lori smiled. "No thanks. I think I'll take a little nap." Her roommate was so outspoken about wanting to "catch" a wealthy man that it was hard to actually criticize her; she was totally open and honest about her pursuit of wealth, almost as if she considered her pretty face and body to be some kind of salable commodity, well worth an attractive, attentive husband's love and loyalty.

"Suit yourself," Julia said, still in front of the mirror. "See you at dinner, Yank." She turned this way and that, gravely regarding herself. "I plan to tell Prince whoever-he-is that I graduated from college with a degree in homemaking. Those men are very macho, you know."

"You're terrible," Lori said, settling herself in a deck chair on the balcony.

But she found herself wondering if, perhaps, she had been able to be as honest about men as Julia was, Paul might not have shown more interest. As it was, she had convinced herself she was not interested in falling in love, and she had said as much to Julia. That must have shown, she reasoned, in her behavior with Paul the night before. Perhaps he found her too independent, too "liberated."

And if he did, it didn't matter, she told herself. She ought to be more social, go downstairs to the lobby or one of the elegant cafés in the hotel, the way Julia did. There were plenty of interesting men around, mostly television and newspaper people, sent here on assigments, and, as Julia had said, there were a few men staying in the hotel who lived exotic lives and who would very likely be interesting to talk to.

The trouble was, she found herself waiting for some more word from Paul.

When it didn't come, when she had bathed, brushed her hair, and penned a cheerful postcard to her parents, she decided to go for a walk. It would be better to walk about in the city than to allow herself to sit around feeling vaguely disappointed, as if she had not been invited to some wonderful feast, as if she had somehow missed out on a party or a parade.

She could see Julia in the lobby, sitting by one of the fireplaces, a glass of wine in her hand, men all around her, as if she were some sort of goddess. To walk by there would probably mean she'd be invited to stop and chat with everybody, to have a drink, to join in the conversation. But outside the city beckoned to her; it lay sprawled like a weary giant, shadows beginning to show themselves in the winding streets. It looked mysterious and somehow enchanting to Lori.

She managed to go through a service door, down a hallway, past the laundry room, and found herself outside in the cool evening, standing on a little porch at the rear of the vast hotel. Somehow she felt as if she had just done something terribly clever by managing to escape those party makers in the lobby.

She walked past the parked trucks that were unloading fruit and produce at the hotel's kitchen ramp, around past the gleaming swimming pool to the street. The lunch with Julia had been light and now she felt hungry. She decided to go back to the stalls and buy some hot bread and smoked fish.

She had bought flowers, a small bouquet to take back to Julia, and a pretty shawl for her mother, when she saw the car. It was hard not to notice it, when one looked in the proper direction, for it seemed to take up nearly the whole width of that ancient street.

It was a Rolls, black and gleaming with rubbed wax, driven by a uniformed chauffeur who seemed impassive to the shouts of children who tried to swarm over and around the expensive car. The car stopped some twenty or so feet from the shawl stand. Then, very quickly, as the chauffeur sat seemingly glued to his position, one of the car's back doors opened and Paul Kardett got out and walked over to where Lori stood.

Her reaction was very mixed; she was, first of all, somewhat embarrassed, since she had the feeling that in this country even to speak to a man on the street was frowned upon. Then she felt surprised, and last of all, a kind of filling, warming sense of pleasure to see him again, to know that he had somehow sought her out once again.

"I hope you'll forgive me," he told her. He reached for and took her hand and briefly held it to his lips in a gesture that seemed totally correct and even charming, as if he had been doing this for most of his adult life. "I'm not going to tell you I just happened by," he said, his dark eyes very warm and admiring, "because that isn't so. As a matter of

50

fact we were parked across the side street from the hotel for quite a long time, Sage and I."

The chauffeur had gotten out of the car, finally, and stood near the car door, apparently ready to lift Lori's packages into the back.

"It's very nice to see you again," Lori told him, her voice a bit nervous, "but why didn't you—that is—"

Paul smiled, taking her arm and helping her into the car. Sage, the chauffeur, apparently understood at once what was to be done; he put the few bundles of Lori's in the trunk, busied himself for a moment in the front of the car, and finally, quite sedately and gracefully, handed Paul a tray containing two glasses of champagne.

"Why didn't I come inside the hotel and call your room?" Paul handed her a glass; it was cool and there was a family emblem cut into it. "Because I wanted to spy on you, I suppose."

Lori looked at him over the rim of her glass. "Spy on me!"

"I wanted to see what magic the city held for you, if any." Paul leaned forward, turning a small switch, so that instantly hauntingly beautiful music filtered out to them —a European waltz. "My mother loved this part of the world. This was one of her favorite waltzes." He settled himself back on the cushioned seat. "She and my father used to dance to it. They'd put music on and at first, they'd be playing, pretending to be at some very important ball, dancing like people out of a movie. But then, after a while, they'd begin to enjoy themselves so much that, as a child, I felt that I was watching something spectacular, something beautiful, watching them waltz." He sipped his wine. "Perhaps," he said quietly, "I was, at that."

Lori put down her glass. There was a sort of shelf that ran across the sides of the car, with places for cups and glasses and even plates. It was an amazing car, with every possible convenience save a bathroom, and Lori wouldn't have been at all surprised if it didn't have that, too.

"Do you always treat your friends this way, Paul?"

"I beg your pardon?"

She had regained some sense of herself, of her dignity, a feeling she had nearly forgotten.

"You said you were spying on me. Were you?"

"I told you—I wanted to see how you reacted to Alexandria's most beautiful time of the day—which is just about now. I wanted to see if you sensed that this is a very special time. I'm glad to see," he told her, in a voice neither serious nor teasing but matter-of-fact, "that you realized that and came out of the hotel. American hotels can be very stifling to one's sense of spirituality." He glanced at her, beginning to smile, as if they had begun to share some private joke. "All those ugly colors someone painted on the walls. And someone had plants flown in from Paris, I understand. Why would they want to do that? We have very lovely flowers here, and in the hills between here and Israel. One has only to go and look."

What he said, Lori realized, was true. Some of the private dining and banquet rooms, plus the main bar (which she had only briefly glimpsed) were painted in colors presumed to give a cool look to a hotel located in a place where it got almost unbearably hot on some days. But the lemon yellows and iced greens had turned out to appear garish.

They were driving down another side street that led to the sea. People sat in dim cafés, under sagging awnings, and stared at the big car as it slowly wound its way along. It was quite dark here; rushlights were on in upstairs rooms and there was the aroma of roasting, spiced meat.

"You love this city, don't you Paul?"

"I suppose I do," he told her. "But then, I am in love with many places. Paris is one. And there's a little fishing village in Italy that I want to go to when I'm very very old and ready to die at last. And of course there is Jerusalem. We used to have a house there, in a grove of trees, but my father got rid of it when Mother died." His hand reached for, and found, Lori's. "Forgive me," he said quietly, "for waiting for you outside the hotel. I should have phoned you, of course. I believe—I believe I was afraid you might not care to see me again." He turned his head to smile into her eyes. "I suppose I would have had to kidnap you, if you'd decided not to ever see me again."

Was he serious? Lori felt her heart quicken. It was entirely possible, she decided, to be a bit afraid of this man, and to realize at the same time his great charm and sheer animal magnetism. She leaned her head back on the seat, closing her eyes, giving herself up to the beauty of the music.

When she opened her eyes, they had left the dismal side streets and were driving along the sea road, toward the brown hills that lay beyond the city. Finally Paul tapped the separating glass and the man called Sage pulled the big car to the side of a somewhat dusty road.

Lori sat up, looking around her; her heart had begun pounding.

"Paul, where are we?"

"Don't be frightened," he told her. "I want to show you something." Sage was opening the door for them. "I want to show you the city from a certain vantage point."

He held her close to him as they walked; his arm was around her slender waist as they walked up a brief hill, then across a meadow to the edge of a path leading back down the other side of the mountain.

The view was sudden and breathtaking. Alexandria was

53

now dressed in her evening clothes, softly glowing with lights, her white buildings bathed in velvet black and purple shadows, so that everything seemed somehow mystical and misty. Lori stood next to Paul, looking down at the lovely old city.

"I think," he told her quietly, "what I'm really in love with is the past. Not only the ancient past, but the past in my own time. My age of innocence, so to speak. Before I knew such evil existed. I—we—used to come here."

"Do you mean you and your parents?"

He looked beyond her. "No. Not my parents. After she—after they died."

Lori did not ask him with whom then, nor did she allow herself to wonder or even speculate as to whether or not he was speaking of a girl, a past, a lost romance. She felt she had no right to ask. Instead she felt a sense of kinship with this strange, sometimes frightening man.

"I felt that way once. Sometimes it's very hard to . . . to reach back into time," she said softly, "and pull out that time of your life when you were really, truly happy."

He turned to her, putting his arms loosely around her, as if to protect her. "Then you aren't happy now?"

She hesitated a second. "I—I don't think it's ever possible to feel that same sense of happiness we felt before we tasted . . . anguish."

His arm seemed to tighten around her. "Anguish? And what has been your anguish, Lori?"

She took a small breath and moved slightly, so that he understood she wanted the conversation halted.

"Everyone grows up," she told him finally. "Paul, are those the flowers you were talking about?"

"Yes. They grow all over the mountains."

She walked down the path a short way, stooping to pick some of the small, peach-colored flowers, holding them to her face briefly to inhale their sweet aroma. From the top of the hill, Paul stood watching her. When she came back up the path, she handed him a flower. He took it gravely, and still holding it in one hand, he pulled her close to him, crushing the flower in his hand, crushing it as he touched her hair, tangling his hands in it.

"Please—"

"Please what?"

She had let her arms drop from around him to her sides. She felt composure come slowly back to her.

"I think I'd better get back to the hotel. We've a meeting—"

He had hold of her arm. "What's wrong? What frightened you?"

She shook her head. "Nothing." But when she looked into his eyes she realized she wanted somehow to tell him the truth, to make things clear and honest between them.

"I don't want to . . . become involved," she said finally, and when he waited quietly, his hand gentler on her arm now, she found herself going on. "I mean I don't want to—" she raised her eyes once more and made herself say the words. "I don't think I care to love someone again. Not just yet."

She thought he might laugh at her, or at the very least become annoyed, but he wasn't either of those things.

"I see," he said, and his voice was surprisingly filled with comprehension. "I understand." And he smiled at her, taking her arm tenderly this time, as they began to walk back to the waiting car. "Now that we're reached some conclusions," he told her, when they were down the grassy hill, "I hope we can have a very enjoyable evening together."

"I don't think—"

"I understand and respect your feelings," he told her, his beautiful eyes candid, "so we will be friends, nothing more.

But first, before we discuss anything more, I want to show you the children."

She stopped walking. "Children?"

"Mmmmm." He took her hand and they began walking again. "Lots of them. All of them very beautiful."

Her heart had begun hammering. It was true; she had not understood him at all. He was, after all, coming from a totally different culture.

"How nice," she murmured.

"I bought them all toys on my last visit," he told her. "Today is the day I plan to stroll through the streets and perhaps buy them some fruit and some flowers."

She felt suddenly out of breath. She climbed into the car and stared straight ahead. How many did he have, she wondered silently. Four? More than four? Maybe a whole lot more. She glanced at his profile. He was probably the most totally attractive male she had ever seen; his hair was softly curly, dark, and his equally dark eyes seemed to hold some deep, black-green shade, like the sea looks very late at night. It was a face she suddenly wanted to sketch.

"Is that sort of thing considered all right here in your country?"

"It isn't my country," he told her. "I consider myself an international citizen." He seemed very serious. "What sort of thing?"

"The children. So, so many of them, that is."

"What's wrong with having a lot of children?"

"Nothing," she said, beginning to wish she'd not started this, "unless we're talking about—how many are we talking about?"

Something, the wry ghost of a smile, was beginning to touch his nice mouth.

"Oh, maybe fifty or so. Give or take a few who grew up overnight and got married or something."

"Fifty!" She sat up straighter.

"Street kids. Beggars, some of them. I try to look after them but there are always more who come along."

"Really, I don't think I care to—"

Suddenly he was grinning. "Mine only by friendship, of course. God himself may care about the many fathers who leave their children to starve on the streets, but not many of the rest of us do. However they manage to live."

"Do you mean there are children out there who—"

"Who are hungry? Yes, of course there are. This country has had many curses put upon it, you know. Hunger is only one of them. But let us talk of happy things. I hope you'll enjoy the children."

She was feeling a vast, overwhelming sense of relief.

"I'm sure I will."

They drove through the winding old streets of the city, and soon, little faces began to peer out of doorways like mice. Finally they got out of the car and began walking, with the children beginning to follow. At first they seemed shy around Lori, but then some of them began giggling, gently tugging at her, and after that they swarmed around them both, hugging, laughing, chattering. Paul gave them money, what seemed like a lot of money, pressing coin after coin into small, dirty, outreaching hands. He stopped at stands and bought sweets and flowers and fruit for them, and boxes and boxes of some kind of candy made from honey and almonds.

Lori stood nibbling on a piece of the delicious sweet; she sat on the ground with ten or so little children who were silently, soberly eating candy, piece after piece.

"I think you spoil them, Paul. Are you by any chance taking care of them?"

"It's hard to do that when they're on the streets this way. When they . . . when they decide to give up, so to speak,

57

it becomes easier. What I'm saying is that, once they're in a home, an orphanage, one can help provide for them."

"I see." She was beginning to understand that this was not the man she had at times thought he might be. If he was a womanizer (and she strongly suspected that he was), he was also a great friend of small children.

But beyond all that she sensed some deep, subtle bond between them. It was not sex, although the attraction between them was sharp, clearly defined, so that eye contact actually caused her to feel some sense of pleasure. What was it?

Whatever it was, she felt a deep sense of oneness, of peace, riding with him once again in the big, chauffeured car.

"Will you have dinner with me?"

Her eyes had been closed; their hands touched gently, there at their sides. She felt completely relaxed and strangely happy.

Too happy, perhaps. Suddenly she sat up, beginning to smooth at her hair, her clothes.

"I'm sorry," she told him, "I can't miss any of the meetings, and I'm not at all sure what's been scheduled for the rest of the day."

"Tomorrow then?" He leaned over her; his face was very close. "We're friends, remember? Friends don't have to lie to one another. Do you want to see me again?"

"I . . . yes. Would you kindly—you're not giving me enough room . . ."

He was kissing her again, very nicely, lingering, tenderly, then with a deep probing. She gave herself up to the joy of her feelings, but not for too long. It was as if some warning had sounded in her.

"You—lied to me!"

"I beg your pardon?"

"I thought you—I thought, back there, when I told you I'm not interested in becoming involved with anybody—I thought you understood. I really did."

"Of course I understood. What're you saying?"

"I'm saying that kissing doesn't go along with friendship."

"What? Friends don't kiss?" He laughed, pleased at their conversation. "Who should kiss then? People who hate each other?"

"I only mean—"

"However, I shall honor your wishes, of course." His eyes were teasing. "You must remember not to kiss me again, Lori."

He leaned forward, tapping on the glass. "The Hotel Teresa."

When she got out of his car, Lori felt that a thousand eyes, all of them peeking from hotel rooms above her, must be watching as Paul bowed, kissing her hand politely. She managed to smile, saying good-bye, and hurry into the busy lobby.

Julia caught up with her as she was waiting for the glass elevator.

"I've been looking all over for you, girl!" Julia's eyes were frankly curious. "At first I thought you were very likely kidnapped in town, and then I decided you'd fallen from that damned balcony you spend so much time on, landed on your head, and had been carted away, unrecognizable."

"I was seeing the sights of the city."

They stepped into the elevator and, after the proper floor had been indicated, were whisked, floating, upward, with the view of the city spread out around them—low white buildings, the marketplace, people everywhere, getting smaller and smaller as they rushed skyward.

"You were, were you? Alone?"

"No," Lori said. "As a matter of fact—"

"I knew it. I want to hear every word. And by the way some reporter from your country is pestering me. I'll probably be asking you to have a word with him."

"Me? I'm sure," Lori said smiling, "you can handle your men problems by yourself."

"Not this one." They stepped out of the elevator and started down the wide, polished hallway. "Let's have a cup of tea and I'll explain. It's only a very small favor, really."

Lori was beginning to open windows in their room; she took off her shoes and blouse, wrapping herself in a familiar, comfortable robe.

"Did you want the bathroom first, Julia?"

"First I want to hear."

"Well, there isn't really that much to talk about. Are there any more staff meetings scheduled, do you know?"

Julia sat on her bed, looking disappointed. "So you don't want to tell me. He didn't make love to you, did he?"

"Of course not!"

"Good. Because after you hear what I have to tell you, you'll think twice before you go too far with him."

Lori turned from the window. She might as well know; if it was anything really terrible, she could tell him she was wrapped up with duties that had to do with the hotel.

"I have no plans to do anything like that. We're friends."

"Oh? Well see that he doesn't start buying you a lot of things. That would be a definite sign."

"A sign of what?" But she was beginning to feel troubled.

"That he's started with you. He's had many affairs, I understand. I told you," Julia said, "I have a little spy who catches me up on everything, and he does it for only five dollars in your American money."

"I'm sure he's had a lot of affairs," Lori said, "he's very attractive." She sat before the dressing table, watching her friend in the triple mirror. "But that's none of my business, after all. We really are only friends."

"Did you know he has all kinds of holdings, not only here but in Europe as well? He's superbly rich, my dear."

"I'm sure he is. Julia, please, I really am not interested in—"

"Furthermore all those ships down at the marina belong to him, part of some huge shipping company he inherited from his father. And by the way your new friend doesn't bother to pay his bills."

"What?"

"It's a custom here, for the very privileged. Money is too gross to be carried about, unless one is giving it away. So the day after Paul Kardett buys whatever it is he buys—like the flowers he sent you, for instance—he sends a servant around to take care of the bill. He was educated at Oxford, but apparently that did little to change most of his attitudes toward life—or women. How did he treat you today, by the way?"

Lori, remembering those sweet, deep kisses, felt her face go suddenly hot.

"He's a gentleman," she said. "A very nice, kind person."

"And charming to the absolute end, I understand. He's a heartbreaker, Lori, used to having his way. He's got a lot of money scattered all over the globe and he can have just about whatever—and whoever—he wants."

"No, he can't," Lori said, heading for the bathroom. "Let me have my bath and change for the meeting and then you can tell me what your favor is."

"How'd you know about the meeting?"

61

"I just guessed we were due for one. I'll be out in plenty of time for you to have a nice soak-bath, okay?"

Julia followed her, leaning against the half-open bathroom door.

"There's just one more thing," she said.

"And what's that?"

"He isn't well liked in Alexandria, in spite of his money."

"But—"

"Oh, he has friends, but they're the close kind, and there aren't many. Did you know he's half Jewish? Believe me, the son of an Egyptian millionaire and a Jewish mother from Paris isn't going to win any popularity contests. Oh," Julia said, arms folded, "there's one more thing, but it might only be gossip."

"I'm sure there must be a lot of that. Apparently," Lori said, "some people make a living out of carrying it around, like—like some kind of dirty laundry!"

"There was supposed to be a girl," Julia was saying, her voice low. "They say he was going to marry her. The girl's father disapproved and something happened."

"What happened?" Lori, still wrapped in her robe, had been sitting on the edge of the tub, waiting for it to fill with the wonderfully scented water.

"She died."

Lori closed her eyes. So that was it, that was what the strange closeness was—it wasn't, as Paul had said, some kind of fate, but instead, the silent recognition of one lonely lover, one solitary person who yearns for someone who is away. That was what she carried within her for Tom, and that was what she had recognized, felt, in Paul.

"I'll go and order tea," Julia said.

Lori undressed and climbed into the tub, letting herself sink deep into it. It was still to be decided, she thought, where they went from here—if indeed their "friendship" went any distance at all. Paul carried secrets, feelings and hurts inside of him that she dared not intrude upon. Still what Julia had told her made her feel closer than ever to him.

She didn't stay long in the tub. Julia was pouring tea, looking a bit upset as Lori went back into the bedroom. A breeze blew in from the sea, mingled with scents from the street beneath them: lemons, strawberries, heady flowers, and sea brine.

The phone rang and the girls both looked at each other.

"This," Julia said, "is where the favor I want from you comes in. I met this, this perfectly horrible man from San Francisco, I think it was, and he's got the idea he can take me out. He's poor as a mouse, except for his job, and he lives in some sort of a room or an apartment over there in your country, with three dogs. Hound dogs, he called them. Please," she pleaded, "tell him I've left the country. Tell him anything."

"I'll do my best, if you're sure—"

"I hate him."

Lori picked up the phone. But the voice that came to her was that of Paul Kardett.

"I just wanted to thank you," he said, his voice low. "I had a lovely day, thanks to you and the children."

"They were charming," she said, very conscious that Julia was there and could hear every word.

"I wanted you to know," he told her, "that the feeling I get when I'm with them—a feeling of peace that seems to escape me everywhere else—I found myself finding again with you. That's really astonishing, you know."

"I-I'm flattered." She glanced rather nervously at Julia, who looked as if she expected to be told every word that passed between them.

"With you," he said, "I felt that goodness, that peace. To tell you the truth, I'm very happy about meeting you."

He has had a lot of affairs, Julia had said.

"Yes," she said, beginning to feel upset, for some reason. "Paul—I can't really talk very well just now."

"Dinner tomorrow night, then."

She looked at Julia, who looked as if she'd just swallowed a mouse and enjoyed it.

"Fine."

She hung up and reached for her hairbrush, hoping to avoid Julia's questions.

"You're very clever, Lori, do you know that?" Julia put a cup of tea in front of Lori, there on the dressing table.

"I don't mean to be."

"Playing hard to get with a man who has as much money as Paul Kardett—"

The phone was ringing again.

This time it evidently was the newsman Julia had been trying to avoid. Lori, tea in hand, went out to the balcony to enjoy it. She sat down, sinking into the colorful pillows of the lounge chair, sipped her sweet tea, and gazed at the green sea beyond.

The sea, in what seemed like moments, had become a shadowed, black-green color, infinitely dark and mysterious.

Exactly the color of his eyes.

Five

Lori slept late the next day; the staff meeting had dragged on into dinner. Everyone connected with the meeting sat at a large round table in one of the dining rooms, eating and listening to the people who had been making speeches make more speeches between courses. The meal was heavy and delicious, and when the talking had finally subsided, Lori realized she wanted nothing more than to crawl into bed.

Now it was a new day, with a slate-colored morning sky and a very light, misty rain. She sat up in bed, stretching, feeling good, feeling some kind of lovely, muted joy deep inside her. Whatever happened to her during the day she felt she could manage and cope with, because toward the day's end, she would once again be with Paul.

There was a moment, in the shower, when she told herself it was wrong to base her day's joy upon the fact that she would be seeing a special man sometime during the twenty-four-hour period. She used to feel that way about Tommy, years before. Even now, in the shower, in almost any shower anyplace, memories would seep back to her about her time with Tom, the time when she was his girl, when they were in love and living; life held no sadness, no horror, only a kind of pleasant sameness, day after day.

Warm, steamy bathrooms scented with cologne and soap always made her think of hot evenings in Chicago, dressing for a date with Tom. Her sisters were both married then, so she was the only girl left at home, and her brothers constantly complained that she took too long in the one bathroom the house had.

It was hard, sometimes, to believe that that was all gone now, all gone and in the past. Now her brothers and sisters all lived out of the state and only wrote brief letters on certain holidays. Her sisters had problems of their own with kids and husbands, and her parents suddenly seemed much older and not so interested in having a big family around them.

I should be married by now, she thought, reaching for one of the towels. I should be married and raising a family, instead of flying to some storybook city and involving myself with a man I'm about as suited for as—

Was Tommy the only man on earth she could have been happily married to?

And how was she so certain they would have had a nearly perfect union? After all her sisters and brothers hadn't achieved that, although a few of them seemed happy enough.

"Hullo," Julia said, when Lori came out of the bathroom. "Did you get it all figured out?"

Lori took down an apple-green dress from the closet and put it on her bed. She smiled at Julia, who, already dressed, was typing up some notes on a pink, portable typewriter.

"How did you know I do most of my worrying under the shower, Julia! You're very clever, do you know that?"

"Apparently," Julia told her, pushing her glasses up on her pretty nose, "I'm not clever enough to avoid running into that rude American newspaperman who seems to spend most of his time in the downstairs bar. He haunts me. Everytime I go to the lobby, there he is, hiding behind one of his newspapers." She resumed typing. "I suppose it's idiotic to get upset over anyone around here, since we'll all be going back to where we came from before long."

Those words stayed with Lori all through the day. There was a staff meeting held in the hotel's clubhouse near the large swimming pool; the press from the bar and lobby had invited themselves, and instead of being boring, it turned out to be rather fun. Lori, about to duck out shortly before noon, had a last glimpse of her roommate chatting away with a very tall, lanky young man in a rumpled suit, who had guided her to a remote corner of the room. He certainly didn't look like the Prince Charming Julia had been searching for.

The girls met again that afternoon, at the pool. Lori was sitting in a poolside deck chair with a book on her lap when, quite suddenly, her friend's capped head bobbed up from the water.

"Come and buy me tea, Lori. I considered drowning myself but I've changed my mind." Julia hoisted herself lightly over the side of the pool, reached for a towel, and flopped in the empty chair next to Lori. "I'm far too beautiful and valuable to die."

"Tea," Lori said, smiling, "means sandwiches, cakes, those little nut pies they have around here, and if I do that, I won't be able to enjoy my evening out. He's taking me to a French restaurant."

"Well, then you'd better go upstairs and put the hair dryer to work. The sun isn't coming out today, you know."

"I know," Lori said. She took the towel from her still-damp hair. "I'll go up in a minute." She turned her gaze from the children at the far end of the pool and looked at Julia. "I've been sitting here thinking about home."

"Homesick so soon, Luv?"

"It isn't that," Lori said softly. "It's only that I feel rather sad because it won't ever be the same again. I had a very nice childhood, a very loving family, and now that's

67

all gone. My folks got old and my brothers and sisters got married and some of them moved—and Tommy died."

"You could have married somebody else, Lori. Don't tell me you couldn't have married somebody else."

Lori closed her eyes. "I suppose I could have."

"But you didn't want to, you see. The point is, you've probably been looking for a different kind of life with a different kind of man, for a long time. Maybe you never really wanted Tom, or whatever his name was, in the first place. Did you ever think of that?"

It was too shocking to even consider. Not love Tommy? Not to have loved him when he loved her so, and now he was dead, dead from a war he hadn't really wanted to go to in the first place.

"I'm going in," Lori said abruptly. "It's getting chilly out here, too cold to swim."

"I'll come with you." Julia picked up her robe. "My father was a printer, you know."

They headed for one of the hotel's side doors. But even as they walked over to it, some reporters began whistling, teasing them.

"No," Lori said, as they ducked up the stairs, "you never told me that."

"We can take the service elevator, I think; come on, Lori." Julia glanced at her once they were safely in the elevator. "They use certain symbols, you know, little markings, printers do. For instance Dad used to write me notes sometimes, and he'd put one of the markings on it. It was always the same one: It meant to turn right side up. That was his message to me, you might say, for me to stay turned up on the right side and not get my life all upside down and wrong and crazy."

"Sounds brilliant to me." The elevator doors closed. Lori

fished in her beachbag for the room key. "Julia, are you sure you're okay?"

"Sure; I'm fine," Julia said. "I just need to get turned right side up again, that's all." She tossed her towel onto her bed and faced Lori. Her eyes were frightened. "I'm beginning," she said grimly, "to think I'm actually falling in love! What a terrible thing to happen with the wrong man!"

"Feel miserable if you want to," Lori told her. "I, for one, am going shopping for a new dress, and tonight, I'm going to have a perfectly lovely time!"

But the gown she bought surprised even herself. She had begun her happy little spree by browsing in one of the new shops on the ground floor of the hotel, where there were discreet showings of totally Western clothing—smart pants suits, cocktail dresses, lovely sweaters, even jewelry, not all of it fake. The prices had been ridiculous, however, and late that afternoon, while Julia kept a date with the reporter from San Francisco (complaining as she dressed for it), Lori found herself in the midst of the outdoor marketplace.

At first she was a bit frightened, and she held onto her purse rather tightly, almost clutching it. But then, as she stopped to buy Julia some fruit, Lori realized how offensive she must seem to those veiled women, as she walked along in her American clothes, holding on to her money as if these people planned to rush at her and rob her.

After that she relaxed and enjoyed her shopping, letting her purse swing from her shoulder. She took off her head scarf and let her long hair tumble around her shoulders. She walked slowly, sucking on an orange she'd just bought, stopping to buy handmade rag dolls for her nieces and nephews and lovely, overly long wooden cooking spoons for all the women she could think of who loved to cook.

69

She bought two for herself, and then she realized everybody at the hotel kitchen back in Chicago would envy her, so she bought a dozen more.

It was getting late, and she had just about decided not to bother with buying a new dress; she really couldn't afford one anyway. She wanted to look pretty for Paul, and yet, some part of her didn't want to see him again and even resented the time taken thinking of him. Julia had said it quite well: They needed to be turned right side up once again.

Going home would take care of all, however.

"Madame?"

Lori heard the voice from a doorway; she stopped and turned around to see if someone was speaking to her.

The woman leaning out the doorway was perhaps thirty—very dark, with lovely, slanted eyes and a fine, straight nose.

"Did you—were you speaking to me?"

The woman smiled, showing strong white teeth. "I have been watching you, madame. You have had a very good time at the marketplace."

"Yes," Lori said, smiling back. "A very good time."

"I can have my son carry your packages."

"Oh, no," Lori said, "I can manage, thank you." She started to go on.

"You would perhaps like to see a dress?"

Once again Lori turned around. "A dress?"

"Yes. A very beautiful one. It comes from Pakistan, from the house of a friend near the Arabian Sea. It has the colors of the rainbow in it."

Lori walked slowly back to the shop. The woman moved from the doorway and went inside the small, dark room. So far Lori had stayed away from the shops, buying only out in the open marketplace. The tiny shops with their mysterious interiors had somehow made her feel a bit frightened.

But now she realized this was a lovely little place.

"Excuse me," Lori said, standing just inside the dim doorway. "But how did you know I've been . . . been thinking about buying—"

"You walk like a woman in love. And a woman in love nearly always thinks of how to please her lover, when she is not with him. When she is with him, she only thinks of him, of course. But away from him—what perfume to wear, what frock to wear—"

"You speak very good English," Lori said, moving into the shop deeper, into the fragrance of it, the restful coolness.

"I went to school in New York for a while. Then I came back here to take over my family's business."

"I see." Lori touched a little carved horse, a horse with wings. The things in here were lovely—carved wooden pieces and mysterious little boxes and all sorts of spices and incense. From somewhere in the back of the store there was the whispering rattle of a curtain strung from pale green beads.

"Here," the woman said, holding out her hand. "Here it is."

The garment seemed to be very fragile and wispy; Lori felt sure it would never fit her, but then, as she held it up, she saw that it was not a dress at all, but rather a length of cloth, cloth as lovely, golden, and peach hued as gossamer wings.

"It is a sari, madame. You would care for me to show you how?"

And so in the end she had bought it for a rather sound price, but it didn't matter, because when she had stood in front of the dim mirror in the back of that shop, and she had looked upon her reflection, she knew something that

until that moment she had not dared to admit to herself:
She was not like Julia or any of the others on this trip.
Alexandria was not only an exciting place to visit and then
leave forever. For her being here was a sort of homecom-
ing—as if she belonged here, at least for a little while.

Some deep, primal feeling, some bond, was holding her
here.

She found Julia wrapped in a warm robe, sitting glumly
in front of the dressing table, brushing her hair.

"That American idiot had the nerve to kiss me—right in
front of everybody in the lobby! He invited me to go for a
ride with him to some old ruins—archaeology, he called
it—and when we got there, all he wanted to do was—" She
stared at Lori. "What *is* that lovely thing you're unwrap-
ping?"

"It's a sari," Lori told her. "And it's magic!"

"It's lovely enough to be," Julia said, gently touching it.
"You'll be gorgeous in that!"

"Thanks. I hope I can remember how to wrap myself in
it!"

She did, or at least, it seemed that she did, so that when
she walked into the lobby, even Paul Kardett, who was
supposed to have had some of the most interesting and
beautiful models in the world as his companions, looked
stunned.

"I didn't expect this," he told her, his voice low and
warm. In the big car, as they drove slowly toward the center of the city, he pulled her into his arms, kissing her as if
he couldn't wait to do so. "In that dress," he whispered,
"your body is more beautiful than ever."

She closed her eyes. Ever since she had gone into that
shop, she had felt somehow transformed, as if the dress

really did have some kind of power to it, as if, by putting it on, she had become exactly the kind of woman this man longed for and needed.

The feeling stayed with her only halfway through the evening. He took her to a very elegant restaurant, near the mosque, a place with slender roses on the tables, white, fine linen cloths and napkins; from somewhere in the back a haunting string instrument played.

He reached for her hand. "There is something I want to give to you. It was my mother's, and it comes from Paris. I think it will suit you very well."

"Paul, I couldn't—"

"Her hands were very delicate, very feminine, like yours," he told her. He bent his dark head and kissed her briefly; his lips felt warm and her heart seemed to stop, then begin to beat harder. "She wore the ring until the day she was killed. She had taken it off that morning, for some reason. I'm sure it will fit you."

"Your mother was killed?"

"Yes, by a land mine. She had driven across the border, you see; she had sisters living in Jerusalem and she was across the border to visit. It was a freak accident; they'd cleared that area, but apparently—"

"I'm very sorry, Paul."

"Yes. At any rate I'd like you to have the ring."

She was about to tell him she would have to give it some thought when suddenly, someone called his name. It was a woman's voice, rather high, perhaps slightly drunk. Lori looked up straight into the flushed face and hard, beautiful eyes of Francine, the girl who had been so nasty at the French Consulate.

"Paul, darling, I've brought Eric with me. You remember him from Monte Carlo don't you?"

73

Paul, obviously not wanting to, got to his feet. "Of course. How are you?"

"He's tired, darling. We can't seem to get a table in here. Since Maxim's burned to the ground, everybody who comes to Alexandria flocks here!" She managed to get a chair wedged in between Lori and Paul. "Now." The cold eyes flicked toward Lori. "Oh, it's you. You mean he's still going around with you?"

"I've got a better idea," Paul said suddenly, reaching for Lori's hand, "you may have the table, Francine. We have an appointment elsewhere, if you'll just—"

Francine's face looked ashen. Clearly she hadn't expected to run into Paul here, and now that she had, she'd hoped to be able to gain some ground with him. To have him walk out on her would spoil her try to get him interested in her once again.

"—I suppose," she said suddenly, her voice rather loud, even in that somewhat busy place, "I lasted longer than any of them. Longer than any of his women did."

"Francine, for God's sake, don't start—"

She turned to look at Lori. "Has he offered you presents yet? Money, an apartment, maybe some piece of jewelry?"

"Paul," Lori said desperately, "I want to get out of here."

"He has, hasn't he? Well, don't worry, little girl, he won't stay long with you. You're too American for him, and wearing that Eastern dress won't change anything. You see, Paul is looking for another Betha, and the girl has to be Eastern and—"

"Talk about her," he said quietly, his face livid, "say her name once more, Francine, and I swear I'll forget that you're supposed to be a woman!"

They were outside in the cool night; he had her hand and they walked quickly to his waiting car. He helped her

74

in; the dress made her a bit clumsy at times because she had to take such short steps. He was silent as the car pulled out into the slow stream of traffic.

"Paul?"

"I'll never go there again," he said. "Not when there's a chance of running into her again!"

"Perhaps we should have stayed," Lori said, her face turned from him. She watched as they came to the highway and began to speed along the sea route. The sea was dark and so was the sky. There were splashes of water from the high waves all along the avenue.

"Stayed! What the devil for? To get so angry with that witch that one finally throttles her?"

She turned to him. "I thought you were lovers. You and Francine."

"Lovers!"

"What, then?"

He suddenly looked uneasy. "And now I must recall all of my . . . indiscretions?"

"Of course not." She suddenly felt upset; the beautiful glow of the evening, the magic feeling she had foolishly thought came from the lovely dress—all of that was gone. "Perhaps you should take me back to the hotel. I'm sorry she managed to upset you so."

He was silent beside her. "Will you come with me?" he asked finally.

"I don't think I—"

"I was going to talk to you about Betha, but not just yet. I'm not sure why." His hand found hers once again and he pressed it tenderly, warmly, to his lips. It was strange, but when this man kissed her hand, she felt as excited sometimes as if he had started to make love to her.

"I told you," she said, "there's no need to go over old indiscretions."

"Betha wasn't that. That's just the point. She was someone very special, very lovely. Like you, in some ways, and yet not at all like you."

Betha. It was the dead girl he spoke of, she felt sure. So he had decided to talk about her at last.

"You asked me to come with you," she said, her voice low. "Where?"

"I have a house—an island—"

"I see." She was hesitating and that was obvious.

"If you're worried about my intentions, I promise you, I only want to talk to you. After all," he said, his voice low, "we don't have much more time, do we?"

Suddenly she felt contrite. "We're friends," she said, "I guess I'd forgotten that. Of course I'll come."

The big car was left at the marina while they were taken rather ponderously in an enclosed, small boat to the island belonging to Paul Kardett. It was larger than Lori had expected, a very private place, with soft brown hills and rambling flowers and a towering, castlelike house.

"It looks," Lori said, "like a place for hiding."

They stood on the boat's narrow deck, facing the island as the boat made its rather laborious approach to a long white pier stretching out from the island.

"Hiding? I suppose maybe it is. I never thought of it that way." He helped her disembark, taking her arm lightly. "This place used to belong to my father. He spent a great deal of time here after Mother died." The house lay ahead of them, situated on a small hill, surrounded by gardens. "Mother had all of those planted. She was very good with living things, a trait not too many women have, although a lot of them pretend to have it." He held open a small iron gate for her. "Mother came from Paris. After a while this island used to bore her."

There was a long flight of stone steps leading to the formal entrance of the old house. Halfway to the top Paul reached from behind and lightly touched her shoulder. She turned around and suddenly he pulled her closer to him. His eyes were surprisingly serious.

"There is an old Arabic proverb," he said, "that tells you if you wish to hide something, hide it in the sun's eye."

So his father had come here to assuage his grief. And Paul—hadn't he very likely done the same?

For the next hour and a half he took her on a grand tour of the entire place, all but the remotest parts of the island. It had been bought by his grandfather, he said, as a present to his fourteen-year-old bride.

"Fourteen!"

They sat on a wide veranda overlooking a courtyard. Below them there was a waterfall that changed colors, green to brilliant yellow, blue to dazzling pink. It was done with lights and the waterfall itself came from a large outdoor piece of masonry that was totally effective. The whole place had a certain quality about it, as if everything possible had been done to make it perfect.

"In this part of the world," Paul told her, "people marry early. If a girl has become a woman, why shouldn't she be allowed to marry? To stay with your partner for perhaps sixty years—that's very good."

Lori sipped the aromatic wine from the chilled glass he'd handed her.

"If you think it's 'very good,' why haven't you done it?"

She was teasing, at least it was mostly teasing, but his face was more serious than she'd ever seen it.

"I almost did," he told her. "The girl died. She was killed by her father and her brothers."

The sudden shock of sadness she felt was totally unexpected. She had, after all, known for certain that someone in Paul's past had died. But this—he was talking about murder!

"Paul—" She leaned over, touching his hand warmly. "I'm so sorry—"

"She was seventeen, the oldest unmarried girl at home." He smiled, his eyes watching the quiet sea. "Betha was very stubborn. She must have refused a dozen men, perhaps many more than that. We used to joke about it, the men who came around to call on her, wanting to court her. We had," he said softly, "a very private world, the two of us."

"I understand."

He was silent for a moment. Lori, sensing his need for this quiet time, said nothing.

"Do you have feelings for the sea, Lori?"

"I—I'm not sure what you mean."

He smiled at her, his eyes showing their sadness. It was as if he had opened a window and, for a little while, his true self, the core of himself, was going to be presented to her. She felt uneasy, even a little dismayed. She had been trying to escape pain; that was one of the real reasons she had come on this trip, to run away from the pain of Tommy. And here she was, about to be engulfed in this man's past horror story!

"I think you do," he said, "and perhaps you are not aware of it. Many women feel a special closeness to the sea and the moon—Betha was one of them. She was far older than seventeen in her mind, you know. She was extremely wise for so young a person."

Lori closed her eyes against the moonlight and the dark sea. Listen, she told herself. Listen to what he has to say, what he needs to say to you. Help him if you can—you may not be able to give him more than just this, to sit here and listen to him and quietly love him.

"We have a deep feeling for the sea here," he said quietly, sitting there next to her in the white wicker chair, holding a glass of wine in his two hands. "We believe that the sea is a time clock, that if you watch it long enough, the waves will wash away all sorrow, all sense of being, so that finally, a peace that cannot be understood will come."

"And has that happened for you, Paul?"

"No," he said, after a few seconds. "Some of us, you see, some of us no longer search for perfect, absolute happiness. There is no such thing here on this earth. Most of us believe and hope that such a life exists someplace else, but to want to be ideally satisfied here is stupidity. Still sometimes I find myself wanting that. Sometimes I even think I may have found it, at least for a few moments. It happens when I'm with the street children." Suddenly he took her hand and held it very warmly, pressing it to his face, his eyes were closed and Lori, watching his dear face, seeing the sorrow there, etched there forever, recorded there until he died, suddenly put her other hand against his face, too. She told herself she must not, must not cry. This man needed no more tears in his life, God knew. He needed sunshine and peace— and love. She realized that his need for love, his capacity for love, was very great.

"I find it," he told her, his voice suddenly thick, "when I'm with you."

"Paul—we mustn't—I'll be leaving soon and we shouldn't—"

"I know; I know. Would you like to see the east gardens? My mother designed them and I had them enlarged for Betha—before she died. They're very lovely in the moonlight."

He held her hand as they left the veranda and began walking through the formal gardens. They were set off by

79

boxed hedgerows; deep inside the garden itself there was a small, screened summer house.

"Betha called it our honeymoon cottage," he said. He held open the door and Lori stepped inside. It was, to be sure, a bit musty inside, as if it had been a long, long time since the windows had been opened to fresh air. But even so it held an enchantment in it, in the elegant, country French furniture, the unexpected European look of the place, the exquisite wallpaper and window treatments.

"It's lovely, Paul. Did, did Betha furnish it?"

"No, although she planned to make some changes, I think. My mother chose the furniture and so forth, on one of her trips to Paris. She made the last one a few weeks before she died." He looked around them. "My father moved into this place and stayed here for almost a month. We could hear him crying out here sometimes, crying and talking to her."

She walked to one of the dormer windows. Outside the silver moonlight lay upon the garden, upon the flowers, like stardust.

"He must have loved her a great deal."

"Yes. She had the wholesome, biblical strength of the eternally good Jewess. Paris didn't spoil that in her." He turned to look at Lori. "It's coming back to me," he said softly.

"What?"

"That feeling of—peace. It's extraordinary, the way you give that to me. It's, it's as if it radiates from you." He came over to her, putting his hands gently on her shoulders. "What is this gift you carry around with you?"

"I'm . . . not sure I know what you mean."

He was drawing her into the circle of himself, into his arms. Lori started to move away, but his arms held her, drawing her closer to him, until at last he was kissing her.

She felt her breath catch in her throat, felt her insides warm with pleasure, and as always she allowed herself the pure pleasure of kissing him and being kissed by him.

"I mean I don't want you to go out of my life. Not just yet."

Not just yet. When, then? When it suited him?

"I couldn't change my plans," she told him, moving, at last, away from him, away from his touch, his hands on her. "In my country one doesn't just change overnight and—and—"

"No? It seems to me that you surely have changed since you came here. You're surprised at that, aren't you?"

"It's true," Lori told him a bit stiffly, "that I didn't—I didn't expect to have such strong feelings about Alexandria. That much is true."

"And is it also true that when I kiss you, you feel as if you never want to leave this place, never want to leave me?"

"No—no—"

"It is true," he said quietly. "I know. I know what you are feeling, how the city can draw you to herself, charm you, and in the end, try to hold you. I have felt it many times—but I always manage to escape her. Did they also tell you my mother's nationality has made it very difficult for us?"

"Yes. I know that."

"And did they tell you of the day when Betha was taken to the hills and shot in the back because she wanted to marry me? Because she was pregnant with my child? Did they tell you how her father walked through the streets with her bloody body in his arms and never once wept?"

"I'm sorry," she said softly. "It . . . it wasn't fair. And when things don't seem fair, it becomes very hard to . . . to accept. But to kill her!"

His voice was low, filled with pain. "I had asked her to marry me that winter. We were in love when the child was conceived; there was no question but that we would be married at once. I had inherited the houses, the ships, the business, the place in France—all of it. It had nothing to do with money. Things like this," he said, "do not happen in your country. But here we try not to speak of them when they happen. But they do happen."

"Perhaps you should leave here."

"Yes, I often do. But the thoughts of her, they go with me." He opened one of the windows and at once a night breeze came in, scenting the place, cleaning it. "Betha's sister left the family because of it. At first we thought they would kill her, too, but instead they disowned her." He took a deep breath of the clean, sweet-smelling air. "Life goes on, they say. Are you ready now for dinner?"

She smiled at him. It was finished, then. He had told her, not all of it—he had not spoken of his feelings for the girl called Betha—but at least he had told Lori a great part of it. Now, in some stronger way, she felt more bound, more tied to him than ever.

Paul had chosen for them to dine not in the huge old house, with its clattering staircases and its echoes and ornate, Eastern furnishings and tapestries, but instead in a small pavilion at the end of the garden, where it was cool, and where the whisper of water spouting from the mouths of seven fish, carved into a fountain, came to them. The food was delicious and delicate, served by a silent old man who wore a turban. There were fruits to be eaten with fingers, breasts of fowl, a clear, pale wine. Beyond them was a lily pond and, beyond that, steps that led to the sea.

After the meal they went inside one of the great rooms, where a roaring fire burned in the huge fireplace.

"Will **you** stay the night here with me, Lori?"

The question was not totally unexpected, but the sudden abrupt way in which it was asked startled her for a moment.

"I—can't do that."

"Can't?"

"I mean I don't want—I told you, I'll be going back home very soon."

"You needn't go if you don't want to."

"Paul," she said, "people don't just throw everything over, toss it out, because a person they scarcely know asks them to! I've a job to go to, parents who expect me to come home with the rest of the hotel people." She looked at him. He sat stretched in front of the fire; the reflected glow made his face seem like the face in an old painting, like that of a soldier, or a handsome, historical hero. "Do women usually do what you tell them to?"

He smiled. "What an odd question."

"It isn't odd at all. Do they?"

"Of course not. Never."

Now it was her turn to smile. "You aren't being honest. At any rate I'll be going back home when the rest of the Hotel Teresa people do, and in the meantime I think I'd better be getting back." She held out her hand. "I've never seen a place like this before. Thank you for showing it to me."

Without another word, without discussing it further, he merely shrugged, picked up the phone, ordered the boat to be brought around, and almost before she wanted it to, it was clear to Lori that her enchanted evening had ended.

They were silent for the most part on the trip back to the marina, and in his car she actually began to feel uncomfortable, as if something had somehow gone wrong between them.

"Paul?"

"Yes, little Yank."

"Don't call me that, please."

"I thought it was a form of endearment to Americans."

She stared out the window. It was quite late now, parts of Alexandria had gone to bed; windows were darkened, sounds—music, voices, cries, even the barking of dogs— had stopped for a while. But in other places lights blazed from late cafés, women strolled the old part of the city, staring at the big car from under dim streetlights.

"You have no right to be angry," she told him, "simply because I . . . I didn't spend the night with you."

"I assure you I am not angry. Merely disappointed."

"It won't help, you know." She had not meant to say that, and yet, once said, she saw that she had struck home with him. "Sex—with another girl—it won't change the way you feel about . . . about what happened to Betha."

"How did you know that?"

"How did I know that you probably seek out some kind of solace in the act of love with other women? I don't know," she told him. "I just sensed it." She raised her eyes to meet his. "I know a lot about you, and I don't understand how I got that knowledge. I just seem to feel things about you."

He touched her face. "You're very sweet, very beautiful. Look," he said, "I'm sorry if I seemed angry with you. But I want you to know that when I asked you to stay with me it wasn't because I wanted to forget for one night. Do you understand that?"

"Yes," she told him. The hotel was in sight now, the night was about to end. From somewhere nearby bakers' early bread scented the air. "Of course I understand that."

But she didn't, and in her heart she felt unspoken words between them. As the car pulled up in front of the hotel and the driver, weary now, held open the door, Paul leaned over and gently kissed her mouth.

"But you would have made the world seem decent; right," he told her quietly. "Making love to you would have changed things for a little while."

So she was right after all. He wanted to hold her, fondle her, kiss her, but only to help his outrage at what had been done to Betha.

And only for a little while.

"Good night, Paul," she said quickly, and she got out of the big car and hurried into the quiet hotel.

There were tears deep inside her, unshed, but she had vowed she would never let Paul Kardett make her cry.

He had said nothing more about his mother's ring, not since Francine had talked about his gift-giving as if it were all a part of some plot.

But then, Lori reminded herself, she never would have accepted it anyway, no matter what.

Six

Lori thought it must surely still be nighttime when she felt herself being urged awake by someone. She sat up; for a brief moment, still half asleep, she had thought she was back home once more, in her parents' house. But it was another time when she was younger, when they were all still living there under that somewhat aging roof, all her brothers and sisters. She experienced a feeling of anger, childish anger.

"Betsy, please stop pulling at me! It isn't time to get up—"

"I'm not Betsy, Luv, whoever she is. I'm Julia, and if you want to take a holiday with the rest of us, you'll bloody well have to get up and dressed and packed!"

The British accent broke through; Lori was awake now. She turned over and, through squinted eyes, peered at her roommate.

Julia was usually asleep long before Lori, and she often stayed in bed long after Lori was up, writing letters or walking the streets of the city, eavesdropping, as it were, on the heartbeat of Alexandria. It seemed very strange to see Julia dressed and looking as if she were about to leave for someplace, when usually one could find her in bed, the pillow over her head.

"Julia, what on earth has come over you?"

"Escape, darling. I'm running away from that crazy American newspaper reporter. Want to come with me?"

Lori sat up, realizing that the lights in the room were on, and outside the moonlight bathed the little balcony. "With you? With you *where*?"

"To romantic Karnak, dearest. We've got a group together, the Teresa bunch and I, and we're flying to Karnak to stay in a perfectly marvelous palace. So come on, get up; we'll have breakfast on the plane."

"You've got to do more explaining than that," Lori told her, swinging her legs to the floor. "Why didn't you tell me before?"

"Before what? Listen, you were out very, very late with your friend, you know. I tried staying awake but I just didn't make it. I should have written you a note, I suppose, but I dropped off to sleep. Anyway, come on now, that's a good girl. I've tossed a few things into a suitcase for you— jeans, sturdy shoes to wear at the tombs."

"To do *what*?"

"The tombs, Luv. We'll be visiting the Valley of the Kings, so you'll want to take something warm, a sweater or something. They say it's cold as death in those places."

Lori realized she was actually getting dressed, pulling on the jeans her friend had tossed to her, looking frantically for her sandals—just as if she could be routed out of bed at any time and told to report for duty!

"Wait a minute," she said, and she sat on the unmade bed. "Would you mind telling me just what is going on here?"

"I did tell you. We've organized a lovely tour, very educational, and it's all free, because our darling superboss is paying for it! He was downstairs in the bar last night, and I think he had a nip too much of Irish whisky. Anyway he started talking about this beautiful place, a palace, right across a valley from the place called the Valley of the Kings. We'll see Hypostyle Hall and—"

"Did I understand you to say, Julia, that you're running away from a mad American man?"

"Completely mad, Luv. He's driving me that way, too. Do you know I actually told him I'm not the daughter of an Oxford professor, that we live in a row house and neither of my parents has ever been outside of London—and he still says he's in love with me! I hate him, and when I heard Mr. Mulvaney talking about the Valley of the Kings, I took a long shot and asked him to treat us all to a little holiday there. It worked."

"Sort of a minivacation within our present vacation, you mean?"

"Exactly. Here, here's your sweater. Put it on and let's go."

Lori opened her mouth to say no, thank you very much,

but she wasn't packed and she hadn't planned on this and besides, she had no reason to run away herself so . . .

But then she realized she actually did have a reason: Paul. He probably would call her; she felt that he would not give up easily. It was very likely that not many women had ever refused him; he had been loved, spoiled, even adored by too many women, it seemed to her. Oh, yes, he would phone, and send more flowers, and take her again to some wildly romantic place deep in one of the most exciting cities on this planet—he would do all of that, and finally, for whatever reasons, she would give herself to him. That was what would probably happen if she didn't do something to reverse things, change something, rearrange something somehow.

This trip might be the perfect answer.

"I'm ready," she announced suddenly. "Let's go. Did you say you've got a bag packed for me?"

"You really mean it? Lovely! But put on your shoes, Lori, or they'll think you're one of the natives!"

It all happened so quickly, and, thanks to the influence of Michael Mulvaney, so smoothly, that Lori didn't have time to think until, sitting next to Julia on the plane, she finally took a deep breath.

"Are you sure you know what we're doing, Julia?"

"Absolutely. Oh, by the way, if you aren't going to eat that sugar bun, I'll have it."

Lori smiled. "It's good to see that the crazy American man hasn't spoiled your appetite!"

"Of course he hasn't."

Lori, spiced coffee swirling in her cup as the plane came into some turbulence, found herself thinking not of the trip, the unexpected minivacation, but instead of Paul. Something, some trick of her mind, took her back to the way his eyes looked when she was very close to him, just before he bent his head to kiss her, for instance. Then warmth would deepen and darken them, so that, instead of the usual deep color of greenness swirling in their depths, there was only darkness. In her mind's eye she once again saw his face crease as he laughed; she thought she could actually hear the sound of his laugh, as if she had walked for days, years, to find that sound—

"Penny for your thoughts, Luv."

Lori opened her eyes.

"No, thank you," she said, and at once she forced herself to think of other things. He probably had phoned her by now, had tried again, had perhaps sent a note by messenger. If she had him figured out correctly, the only way he could rid himself of his anguish was in another woman's arms. Only then was the memory of his dead lover erased.

But it came back again and again, so that always he was seeking love, seeking that connection with another that would rid him of the horror of what had happened to the beautiful girl who carried his baby.

There they were again, the tears behind her eyes. Such a man as this needs love; it is his lifeline.

But how could she give him that, when she would be leaving so soon?

The Old Winter Palace had been built in 1906, and its furnishings reflected that era. It was a lavish mixture of Eastern and Western styles; there were shining brass lamps that looked as if they contained genies and carved tables that had been made in Racine, Wisconsin, and everywhere the pungent aroma of incense. It was lavish to the point of reminding both Julia and Lori of something out of a late-late movie, a fact which one whispered to the other on the way to their suite.

There was a breathtaking view from their room, so much so that Julia could hardly pry Lori away from the window when it was time for them to meet downstairs for dinner.

"The temple of Karnak has been around a long time, Luv. It will still be there after dinner, I'm sure."

Lori and Julia were seated at one of the round tables in the great dining hall, along with the hotel managers from Chicago and New York, plus several people from the Alexandria Teresa. The conversation drifted to the myths, or historical fact—whichever way one cared to accept it—regarding various dead kings.

"We've all heard of young Tut, of course," someone said, a dark-eyed, polite young man who shared their table. "But there's another story that carries an even more interesting love story. His name was Nella, and he was perhaps forty when he died—rather a long life span at that time. His queen was middle aged, too; they had been together since they were children, although they were separated some time around 1300 B.C. Then, according to what we've been able to find out, he went to fetch her, against his family's orders. They were renegades, those two, living only for each other. When Nella's wealth and crown were restored to him, he and his queen no longer wanted it. They had lived too long in the peace of the wilderness, eating wild locusts and honey."

Later, when they'd unpacked the few things they'd brought and were back in their suite, Lori talked about the rebel king and queen.

"Why do you suppose they were the way they were, Julia?"

Julia was sitting on one of the two antique beds, which was covered with an intricately woven throw of some sort, very Eastern and warm. The night had come suddenly, the turning out of a light, it had seemed, and now it was cold outside the warmth of their rooms.

"How did they get to be king and queen, you mean? I don't think they were elected, Luvvie."

"I don't mean that, I mean, what do you suppose made them not care about everything they had—all the jewels and land and—"

"Bloody crazy, if you ask me!" Julia began carefully plucking her brows, peering rather nearsightedly into the mirror on the lid of her makeup case. "Now if I were to be reincarnated, I'd like to come back as a very pampered someone who owned fabulous jewelry and lovely clothes and thousands of acres of land. Why was this woman satisfied to chew on nuts and live in the woods with her man? Like I said—she must have been looney tunes!"

Lori stretched out on her bed, which was really more like a soft, elebarote couch. "I think I know why. It was because they loved each other so."

"I wouldn't have to move to the bloody woods to show how much I'm in love," Julia said, wincing as she used the tweezers. "Give me the palace life any day."

"But don't you see, Julia? Being together was what mattered; loving each other was what mattered. The rest of the world didn't."

"Well, they don't sound like very responsible people to me," Julia told her. "Do you know I think I'm blinding myself with this torture instrument?"

"Responsible. That's such a terrible word!" Lori leaned back against the soft cushions. There were gardenia plants in the room; the place was deeply scented with that sensual fragrance. "Responsibility killed Tommy."

The words slid out of her mouth almost before she knew it. She had not meant to think or talk about him on this trip.

91

"Do you know what I think, Lori? I think you're confused about some things. I mean, I don't think people can just chuck their lives, run away and forget who they are and what they are. God knows I've tried doing that, but it never really works. If I really like the man, or if I suspect I might be falling in love with him, I always tell him the truth about myself." She reached over and patted Lori's hand. "And if your Tommy died doing what he thought was his responsibility, then he was a real hero, wasn't he? We've had our share of heroes at my house, believe me. My grandfather died at Dunkirk because he happened to be a responsible person. He was in his little fishing boat, trying to get those poor doomed British soldiers out of the water, when gunfire just blew him away." Her face had softened. "I never knew him, but I think about him a lot. When I have a son, I'm going to call him James, for Grandfather."

Suddenly Lori wanted to speak from her heart. Perhaps it was that she had never before seen that special tenderness in her roommate's face; usually Julia was somewhat abrupt and even cold in her evaluations of people and events, but now, her pretty blue eyes looked misty.

"Julia, aren't we trying to . . . to trick ourselves?"

"What?"

"Trick oursleves into not thinking about the people we want to think about most. I'm sure you came here for basically the same reason I did—to run away from a very worrisome man, right?"

Julia was suddenly very busy rummaging in her little makeup kit.

"Wrong. I, I came here to see the tombs and the Hypostyle Hall."

"Julia, you aren't being honest with me."

Julia let her breath out. "I told you that Yank scribbler

was driving me crazy; I never made a secret of that. Of course I'm running away from him, but it's because he's a lunatic, not because I'm madly in love with him!"

"I don't believe you, " Lori told her smugly. "I happen to believe that at long last you've fallen in love, not with a man's money or his power—the things you always felt sure would turn you on—but with the man himself! And you're scared to death, because he's—"

"He's crazy and poor and he lives across an ocean from where I live and want to go on living," Julia said, her voice low. "Yes, Luv, it's true. I'm in love with him, and being in love is just what I thought it would be—torture!"

"It isn't supposed to be, you know." Beneath them in the palace courtyard came the sound of a romantic violin. "And yet," she said, "one can't help thinking how lovely it would be to be here with the man one hates."

"Oh, don't you like my company, is that it?" Julia got up and peered out the window. "Who is that down there, sawing away on that violin? Do people always pop out of nowhere in this country and start serenading you?"

By this time Lori had joined Julia at the window. "Do you suppose we can call down requests?"

Suddenly they were both giggling like schoolgirls. This minitrip, Lori realized, had been good for them after all.

So they stood there listening, and after a while the music seemed to become a part of that chilled night—a black sky filled with crystal bright stars, the deep valley where the dead kings lay with their queens, the mountains beyond.

"Julia?"

"Yes, Luvvie?"

"I don't . . . want to go away, go back home, and never see Paul again."

They had turned out the light in the room, so that only the brilliance of the night lit it, covering the walls and furniture and rugs and couches with a soft, blue-white glow.

"I know you don't," Julia said kindly. "To tell you the truth, I feel the same way about Link. Isn't that a Yank name for you, though? At home I dated men with names like Neddie and Roland and Jack, and even Sir Stewart, and then I meet my true love and he's a dammed Yank all the way through!"

"I want to . . . to have a little time with him," Lori said, her voice almost a whisper. She turned from the window to face Julia. "I'm going to be very irresponsible and give myself whatever little time there is left, before we go back home. I'm going to be happy and try to help him be happy for a little while. Because," she said softly, "I don't think he's had one really happy moment in a long, long time. I can do that. I can do that for him, at least."

Suddenly Julia's eyes were worried. "You might do well to think a bit about that," she said. "Leaving will be hard enough without having too many memories to take with you."

"But don't you see," Lori said almost eagerly, "that's exactly what I want! I want to have a thousand sweet things to remember when I'm back home, Julia! I want to have them all stored away someplace inside me, so that when I'm home and I'm away from him forever, I'll be able to take them out of myself, out of my heart, like little treasures; I can live that way. I can get through it all that way. But I, I have to have something!"

Julia put her hands up in horror. "Of course you do; of course you do! You're a woman, Lori, even though you don't seem to realize that!"

"I know I'm a woman. And because I am, I want to be in his arms, to give myself to him—to make him happy for a little while! I didn't think I could let myself be one of his women, but now, I know that's what I ought to do, what I should do!"

"Lori! I honestly believe the desert air has made you lose your mind!" Julia's voice was earnest. "Now you listen to me: Of course you deserve love, the ups and downs and upsidedowns of love. And I suppose it's lovely for a while, or at least different, to have one's life turned the wrong way, down side up, like the little printer's sign. But one can't go on like that forever, you know, and at best, that kind of feeling can be just the opposite from what you're hoping it will be."

"Are you telling me that I shouldn't let Paul make love to me when we get back to Alexandria?"

"I'm telling you that you deserve much more than—than just being one of his conquests! Even if you love him, you deserve much more than a few nights with him and a lifetime of memories, no matter how lovely those memories might happen to be!" Julia smiled at her. "I'm sure, down deep, the fact that you actually are a responsible girl will save you."

"Save me! Julia," Lori said, beginning to smile, "you really are a very old-fashioned girl, do you know that?"

"Of course I am. And so, my love, are you."

And so they slept, in the near shadow of the three-thousand-year-old tombs, where kings, young and not so young, lay wrapped in linen and spices, preserved by the ancient art of embalming and mummifying. Some of the tombs, as the girls discovered the following day, had been wrenched open and desecrated, but others were still untouched, sealed shut against time and worldly evil.

Sometimes everyone in the party had to lean over to go from chilly room to room, guided by the torchlight their guide carried. To Lori it was a very special experience, as if time stood still for a little while.

"Awesome, isn't it?" The woman who spoke was also staying at the Old Winter Palace; Lori had noticed her dining alone that morning, sitting by a window in the ornate dining room, sipping coffee and looking fit and not at all lonely. "This is the ninth time I've been through these tombs here in the valley. Something always brings me back. Cigarette?"

They were outside the tombs, lounging about under some olive trees. Some of the people were busy taking pictures while others, glad to be out of the sun's intensity, simply sat on the cool grass and fanned themselves.

"No thank you; I don't—"

"Oh, it isn't tobacco, dear. I wouldn't dream of smoking that stuff. It's herbs—rosemary and fennel, things the ancient kings used to snuff up their noses. You're from the Midwest, aren't you?"

"Yes, Chicago. And you—you're an American, aren't you?"

"Is that surprising?"

The older woman took off her sunglasses. She was perhaps fifty, with crow's-feet around her eyes, steady gray eyes over what was probably a very beautiful face at one time. There was still a certain beauty about her, a kind of merriment that came into her eyes as she surveyed Lori.

"I didn't mean that," Lori said quickly. "What I meant was—well, I'm glad to talk to someone from home besides the people I work for." She put out her hand. "I'm Lori Coleman, here with the Hotel Teresa people."

"Doctor Stephanie Palmer, with what used to be Good Shepherd Hospital."

Lori looked at her quickly. Yes; it was only a little surprising to learn that this attractive woman was a doctor. She didn't seem like the usual tourist; Lori had seen a few of them wandering around in Alexandria, looking as if they'd just come from a hardware convention someplace.

"What used to be?"

"We had a rather bad fire last month. Have you ever been in a fire?"

"No, thank God." Lori looked around her. Julia seemed to be asleep on the grass, with a newspaper over her face. "We've only been here since last Tuesday, so we didn't read about it. I'm terribly sorry."

They were walking into a pretty grove of fig trees, where there were benches and a small, old-fashioned well. They both took turns getting drinks, cupping their hands when the bucket came all the way up.

"The children weren't hurt, thank God—we got them out first. Then we tried to get the rest, all the adults. We ended up with a patient with one broken leg having two, when the dust cleared, but no fatalities."

"That's a blessing. Doctor Palmer," Lori said, "do you mind if I ask you something?" She stared into the cool blackness of the old well.

"Of course not. Frankly I've been hoping to meet another American for some time. We use the house for a hospital now, and it gets very hectic, because we treat about two hundred walking patients a day. Sometimes I just—run away. I come over here to the valley and walk through the tombs and finally my soul gets calmed and I'm ready to go back."

"I wanted to ask you about—how you feel about being here, living here, giving up your life the way you must have. Is it terribly hard to turn your back on your life?"

The doctor smiled, grinding out her herb cigarette, picking up the remains of it and tidily dropping them into her purse.

"Not at first. I didn't think I had much of a life, you see.

97

I come from Cape Cod, a place called Barnstable. Do you know it?"

· "People in my family don't travel much."

"Well, it's a nice enough place to live. My father was a doctor there. He died the semester I was graduating from med school, so I guess I felt—"

"As if you could make a choice?"

"Yes."

"And," Lori persisted, "do you find yourself missing the Western world?"

"If you mean do I long for the taste of a genuine hot dog, no, frankly. I miss my parents, and the house I grew up in, but my life is here now." Suddenly she smiled wisely at Lori. "You've been caught up in it, haven't you? The magic of this place—the mystery of the Middle East—has caught you in it's hold, hasn't it? You might grow to be very old, my dear, but I promise you, you'll never forget the hills, or the olive trees and the flowers and the look and smell and excitement of this part of the world. That happens to some people, you know. We belong here, even though we weren't born here. They tell me I lived here once before, in another life."

"And," Lori asked, "do you believe that, Doctor Palmer?"

"Sometimes. Come on, dear. I think they're calling us. It's time to go back to the palace."

Lori and Julia had dinner in their suite that evening; apparently Mr. Mulvaney had been rather badly sunburned during the day and the evening festivities were canceled out of a kind of "relief and regret," as Julia put it.

"I can't imagine what that bird is we're eating," Julia said, reaching for another tiny leg. "Too big for a sparrow. Do they have robins in this part of the world? I hope I'm not eating a robin."

"A pigeon, more likely. They're a delicacy around here." Lori almost smiled but managed not to.

"A *what*?"

"Julia, you eat fried chicken in London, don't you?"

"Only in those horrible fast-food places that copy yours! Anyway I'm quite filled up, thank you. Do you know what that insane American newspaper man told me? He said I'm built to have babies. Isn't that telling me I'm a potential brood sow?"

"I think it's telling you he finds you very attractive." Lori was lying on her couch on her stomach. From here she could gaze out the window at the black, star-studded sky. The stars seemed bigger here, closer; it was easy to see why fables were born, why stories were spun about the earth and sky—they seemed almost to be one at times.

"Well," Julia said, her voice once again cool and practical, "when I start spawning, you can bet the man will be rich and British. I'm a cricket-by-the-hearth if you want the truth of it. Only I'd like my hearth to be placed in a very large, expensive country house, thank you."

And so nothing had changed for Julia, it seemed, but Lori sensed a new kind of confidence within herself, so much so that when the group went shopping the following day, in Karnak, she splurged and bought herself a beautiful caftan in shades of green, from dark to lime.

"You bought that to wear for Paul, didn't you?" Julia's voice was flippant, as usual, but she looked concerned. "I suppose you plan to throw yourself at him as soon as we get back; am I right?"

"Something like that."

Just thinking about seeing him again, talking to him in a new and different way, a way that didn't hide what she felt for him—thinking about that gave her such a feeling of happiness that she felt almost astounded.

"You're just dying to go back home with a broken heart, aren't you, Lori?"

"It isn't that. It—"

"I still think people ought to behave responsibly," Julia said. "Suit yourself."

What, Lori wondered, as she followed the others through the vast, cool rooms of the great Hypostyle Hall, was it that had changed her ideas about her relationship with Paul? At what point had she discarded the facade of friendship and gladly, joyfully, accepted the mantle of love that was both sensual and spiritual? She wasn't sure, but the discussion they had that night on the island, when he told her of the murder of Betha and their unborn baby, certainly had something to do with it.

And so whenever some small warning sounded in her mind, whenever the thought crept in and she saw herself loving him for years to come, never seeing him again, just going about her boring life in Chicago, a girl in love with a man who probably never thought about her—she shoved the thought aside.

She was standing outside, in the shadow of the great building, when Doctor Stephanie Palmer walked through one of the wide entrances and waved.

"I didn't know you were with the group," Lori told her, "how nice to see you again!"

For some reason she found herself admiring this calm woman who had apparently chosen to practice medicine in Egypt.

"Oh, I'm not with the group," the doctor said. "I came here alone, as I often do when I'm worried. I find a sense of peace here."

"Doctor Palmer, may I ask you something?"

They walked along together. "Of course, ask away."

"Do you ever miss living back home? I mean, do you ever miss—"

"The Western way of life? Yes; I suppose I do, sometimes. Although it isn't quite as simple as yearning for apple pie a la mode when you can have baklava with nuts here. Do you follow me?"

"I'm not sure," Lori said, smiling. "I understand that one often gets the feeling in this part of the world of . . . having lived a life here before."

"The Eastern people, including the Christians, have a rather startling view of things, if that's what you mean. They believe that there is evidence of reincarnation everywhere—in the rebirth of trees, for instance. One comes to adjust to their beliefs, that's all."

It was the colors of the land that held her spellbound, she decided, as she looked toward the dry brown hills beyond. There was a kind of beauty to their starkness, to their golden-burnt color.

"Perhaps," Lori said slowly, "home would seem sweeter if one only had to think about it at times, and not live there. Do you understand what I mean?"

"Of course. But that's running away from something, isn't it? No, my dear, it's not fond memories that keep me here. It's a feeling I have that I belong in this corner of the world. The hospital is my life, and I expect I'd be uncomfortable back home. People think differently here, you see. There's a vast difference between the Western way of thinking, reasoning, and the way an Egyptian or Jew or Moslem thinks. We—I don't say *they* any longer—have traditions, ancient rituals, beliefs stemming from ancestors who lived two thousand years ago in the same cities: Cairo, Karnak, Jerusalem. It isn't quite the same as living in Chicago or New York or Boston." She peered at Lori from behind her festive sunglasses. "Are you by any chance involved with a

101

man here? Forgive me, but I sense some rather desperate quality in your question."

"Yes," Lori admitted. "There's a man. I've just about made up my mind to try to make him as happy as I can, while I can. I know, I know that may sound foolish, especially since I'm in love with him, and I know I'll probably suffer for a while, but I'll come around. It has to do with wanting to take away his sadness. Do you understand?"

"By sleeping with him, you mean?"

"Not only that," Lori said quickly. "By loving him completely, for the time we have left together."

Stephanie tilted her head a bit, looking at Lori. Her intelligent eyes narrowed behind the sunglasses.

"Do you actually want to be hurt, my dear? Lori, don't feel guilty for whatever it is that makes you feel guilty. Guilt is a real killer, you know. It does terrible things to people, eats them alive, breaks them."

Lori's voice was firm. "I don't feel that way. I've nothing to—"

"There's my taxi," Stephanie said suddenly. She picked up a small valise. "I'm on my way back to the hospital. You must come and visit some time and we'll talk again. Good-bye, my friend." She held out her hand.

Lori extended hers. "Good-bye."

When she had packed up and she and Julia were riding in the taxi to the airport, Julia suddenly turned and looked at Lori.

"Who was that nice-looking lady you were talking to? Is she American?"

"Yes. She's a doctor."

"Well, I couldn't tell that, but I could certainly tell she was a Yank. You've all a certain look about you, you know. Healthy as cows."

Lori smiled. "Thanks a lot."

"Well, since we'll be leaving before too long, why don't you invite her to come to Alexandria? She seemed like a pleasant sort."

"I doubt if she would," Lori told her. "She's terribly involved with her work at the hospital."

But still she found herself wondering if she would ever see Stephanie Palmer again. There had been practically no time in which to talk, to speak of the things that were uppermost in her heart. Somehow she felt Doctor Palmer could help her control her wild feelings concerning Paul, that both as a woman and a doctor she would understand Lori's feelings about this part of the world, so real, so strong that she almost dreaded leaving.

"I know what it was," Lori said suddenly, on the plane back. "I know what it was about Doctor Palmer that fascinated me!"

"Well, she'd have to be very bright, and all intelligent people are fascinating in some way, I think. So—"

"No," Lori said, "it wasn't that. Julia, it was because she feels she belongs in this part of the world, that's why I felt I wanted to talk to her! Some change came to her, something that turned her mind to a different way of thinking—it was the mind change that I wanted to talk about!"

Julia's eyes clouded. "Are you feeling all right, Lori, Luv? Seriously I've had the strangest feeling that you're about to come to some decision that is going to knock us all flat. I don't know what it might be, but I wish you wouldn't!"

"I don't know what you're talking about," Lori said, and she immediately closed her eyes, ending the conversation.

But she did know, and Julia's suspicions were true. Lori *was* going to make an important decision, and if it went the way she thought it probably would, it was going to shock everybody who knew her, just as Julia said.

She was thinking of asking for a transfer to the Hotel Teresa in Alexandria. And from there to the new, half-finished Teresa due to open soon in Tel Aviv. Something of this part of the world had been planted in her, and more and more she yearned to stay.

How much of all of this Paul had to do with, she did not know, or care.

Seven

When the group landed at the airport and Lori stepped out of the plane, she suddenly saw herself facing the blue sea with the city of Alexandria spread about her, low white buildings crouching along the seaside in the blazing sun.

Once again that odd feeling of something close to joy washed over her. There were no staff meetings, no formal parties scheduled for this day, so if she wanted to she could lounge about in the cool room at the Hotel Teresa or else sit on the balcony, calmly watching people going to and from the marketplace. Or she could lose herself in the heartbeat of the city, walking in it, sensing its mystique.

"I want to go home to London," Julia said suddenly, as they were unpacking. "I'm bloody tired of taking things out of a suitcase and putting 'em back in again. I'm ready to go home; enough holiday for me, thank you!"

"It's another week, Julia. Relax."

That was what Lori did, for the rest of the day. The phone rang three times; the first time she was in the shower, washing the desert sand out of her hair. She opened the shower curtain just a bit, listened, and realized Julia was talking to someone, her mad Yank, probably.

Julia was standing by the balcony door when Lori came out, drying her long hair with a towel.

"You answer it next time, please," Julia told her. "Do you know what Link told me? He said if I don't meet him downstairs, he's going to get horribly drunk and he'll probably lose his job, because he's due to call his editor tonight and give him a story over the phone."

"He's in love, poor thing," Lori said, smiling.

"But he can't be!" Julia's face was almost white-looking. "He mustn't be! It's all wrong for us!"

"Julia, I've never seen you like this before. Look, you could go down there for a minute and—"

"A minute! It takes that man five minutes to stop telling me hello." She shook her head. "No, thank you. It's my turn in the shower."

The phone rang again, and this time Lori answered. She thought it might be Paul; he should have called before now.

Should have?

If he really cared, that is.

It was Link on the phone, slightly drunk, wanting to talk to Julia.

"She's in the tub, I believe."

"Good. Tell 'er I'll be right up."

"I'll tell her you called," Lori said. "Good-bye."

"Wait," he said quickly, a note of worry creeping in. "Tell her—tell her I'm offering her one of the most beautiful sunrises in the world—the view over the Golden Gate. Will you tell her that?"

"Sure," Lori said, "I'll tell her."

She did, and he called again. While Julia talked into the phone, Lori made herself comfortable on her bed, with writing paper and pen. There were letters to write; she had to tell her parents so many things, but it seemed to her to be better to call and talk to them.

"All right," she heard Julia say finally. "Ten minutes and no more, and I'm bringing my roommate with me!" She hung up and looked at Lori helplessly. "Will you go down with me for a few moments? He says if I don't he'll jump in the deep blue sea, and I think he means it!"

Lori hesitated just a second. She glanced at the phone and then back to Julia. "Sure," she said good-naturedly, "I'll be right with you. Just let me get out of this caftan." She'd bought it at Luxor, at the airport, when the plane had stopped to refuel. She had shopped everyplace they went, buying several of the long, free-flowing gowns, all in exotic patterns, all in rich, beautiful multicolors.

All to please Paul.

"Wear it," Julia urged. "You look marvelous in it." She gave Lori a look of quick compassion. "Did it ever occur to you that Paul Kardett is a different breed from my little-boy newsman down there? I don't imagine Paul takes to rejection kindly, Lori. In fact judging from what I've heard about him, I'll wager you're the first girl to ever turn him down!"

"You mean you think that's why he suddenly doesn't appear to care whether I'm dead or alive?"

"I mean," Julia said, "that's the reason why he suddenly doesn't appear, period. You've hurt his bloody feelings."

"I feel rather foolish," Lori said quietly. "I was all decided to try to love him, to comfort him, and now he doesn't call me!" She felt lightheaded with some kind of muted hurt and disappointment. "Come on, Julia, let's go downstairs, meet your wacky friend, and have ourselves a ball!"

Julia's "wild Yankee" greeted them as soon as they

walked into the dim downstairs bar. It was an American version of some sort of Persian den, according to Link, who seemed to think that was extremely funny.

"Julie and I are getting married," he told Lori, his face very serious, "only she doesn't know it yet." He was a good-looking, boyish young man with a charming smile and a nice way of peeking at people over his glasses. He was not, however, exceptionally handsome or witty, and he certainly wasn't rich, since Julia ended up buying him a sandwich.

Lori, sitting there with her grape juice untasted in front of her, found herself wondering again about Paul. Was it possible that he could let her go this way, thinking he'd never see her again? Could a man look at a girl the way he'd looked at her, his eyes filling with warmth and desire, and simply forget her, and go on his sorrowing way as if she made no difference to him at all?

Apparently.

When three men in their thirties or so joined the table, Lori found herself listening to one, smiling, nodding, and generally managing to act as if she were enjoying herself. She wasn't flirting, but she knew it was a sham, all the same, a dishonest sham, to sit there and act as if she thought that what that nice man was saying—something about the import-export business—was interesting. Maybe it was, but just then she was feeling a vast sense of loss, a quiet, steady sadness.

Paul was gone, gone out of her life.

She really thought he was, so that when, opening her mouth to smile at something the man next to her had said, she suddenly saw Paul standing in the doorway watching her, she felt stunned. Her heart seemed to stop, then begin a slow, steady thudding.

He was clearly waiting for her to make the move, to come to him.

107

Lori let her breath out. "Excuse me," she said softly, and gathering up her purse, she left the table, or started to.

The nice man in the export business grabbed her arm. "Hey, don't leave!"

"Sorry," she told him. "It's very late. Thank you and good night."

And she walked across the room, straight to Paul. A hint of a smile touched his mouth as he looked down at her.

"Are you ready to go?"

"Go? Where?"

"To the street festival, of course. It's very beautiful and very significant." His voice was calm.

Lori glanced rather nervously toward the table, where Julia, Link, and the rest of them sat watching.

"Yes," she said finally. "Yes; I'm ready."

Night had come; there was a crusty sky and drifting night clouds.

"The car is just over there," he told her. "Unless you prefer to walk."

"I'd rather walk." She took a deep breath as they left the hotel. "I suppose you know you frightened me," she said, looking straight ahead as they walked along.

"I? I frightened you? I hope you aren't afraid of me."

She stopped walking. "Paul, surely you know when you don't . . . when you make a woman feel that you . . . care for her and then you don't get in touch with her—" She felt her face color. "Never mind," she said, "it doesn't matter."

"But it does matter!" He touched her face gently, standing close to her. "It matters very much what you feel about me."

She suddenly decided not to tell him. To be in love with

him was one thing; to talk about it was something quite different.

"Did you say we're going to a festival?"

"Stop changing the subject," he told her. "Now, why were you afraid?"

"I was—it wasn't exactly—" She let her breath out. "Okay. I was afraid I'd never hear from you again."

"But—" he looked astounded. "I thought that was what you wanted! I thought, when I phoned and they said you'd gone off on a holiday with your friends, that was your way of telling me you didn't want to have anything more to do with me!"

"You thought that and you still came looking for me?"

He smiled at her. "Of course. Do you think I give up someone dear to me that easily?"

His words set a tone for their evening. Lori had not been forced to admit her real feelings and how strong and deep they were, and how uneasy those feelings made her, in view of the fact that Paul was still in love with, and in mourning for, a dead girl. But for now, for tonight, they seemed to have mutually agreed not to talk of death and parting, of sadness and heartbreak, but instead to be like children, children holding hands, walking down twisted, half-dark streets, until at last they came to Tatwig Street, where the long, winding procession was already in progress.

People walked along singing and chanting, cymbals were sounded, bells of various sizes and sounds rang as they walked along. There were girls carrying flowers, children scattering rose petals; everybody seemed to be smiling. From time to time, as they walked along, the sliver of a moon came out behind the low clouds, lighting up faces, making things sharp and clear. All around her were the mingled sounds and smells she'd grown to cherish—crushed chrysanthemums, strawberries, roasting pigeons, sea-washed air.

Paul stopped in front of a mosque and suddenly, leading her to its arched doorway, he pulled her into his arms and kissed her warmly.

"Thank you for giving me this night with you," he told her. "I don't imagine you can understand how I felt when I phoned you and they told me you'd gone off someplace. I thought what I'd told you about my past may have driven you away from me."

She leaned against him. There in the winding street, lovers walked with the great crowd, their arms around each other. Across the street Lori saw a tall young man stop, pull a girl from the procession, and kiss her there on the street. She laughed, throwing back her head; her dark hair trailed down her back.

"A prostitute," Paul said. "This part of town is filled with them. Come on," he told her, "perhaps I shouldn't have brought you here after all."

"Paul," she said. "Wait—I've got something to tell you."

His dark eyes were steady. "I don't want to talk about your leaving, if that's what it is. Besides, no matter where you go, I can always find you, my friend. Your Chicago isn't all that far away, you know."

My friend. Lori reminded herself of their friendship. He had asked nothing more from her than that—friendship and the closeness of kisses.

"Paul," she said, over the din of laughter, talk, and shouts from the parading people, "I think I'm going to stay."

"What? I can't hear you."

"I said I think I'm going to stay on. If there isn't an opening for me at the hotel here, I'm fairly sure there will

110

be when the new one in Tel Aviv opens. I want to stay in this part of the world—for a while, anyway. I'm afraid," she said, "I've fallen in love with it."

"Stay? You're going to stay on here?" He looked stunned. He did not, she realized, look happy or even pleased. "You mean you aren't going back when the others do?"

"I haven't spoken to anyone yet," Lori told him. Some kind of pain began inside her, totally unexpected. Without really realizing it, she had thought Paul would be glad, happy that she might not go home so soon. "I . . . I'm still not certain of course," she said rather uncomfortably.

"I see." They began walking again. This time he did not hold her hand or put his arm around her protectively. "I suppose you know it might not be safe always," he told her. "There has been war in this part of the world for many years now. Fighting, skirmishing, off and on. It isn't always safe for a woman alone."

Lori raised her chin a bit. "I won't be alone; I'll always have my friends who work at the hotel." He was, in effect, telling her he wouldn't be seeing her again! Where was the pleasure she had thought would come into his face? He looked grim and somehow solitary, walking along beside her in the busy, narrow street. From time to time people from the long procession bumped into them, laughing, pushing them, trying to get them to join hands with the others who danced through the streets.

"Let's get a drink someplace," he told her suddenly. "We need to talk."

Suddenly Lori realized she did not want to be there. Moments before she had been caught up in the mystique and excitement of the celebration; she had felt a part of that great, throbbing heartbeat that was the city, but now she felt close to tears. They stood on Tatwig Street; the tombs lay ahead of them.

"I think I've had enough, Paul. So many people—"

Tables had been set outside the cafés so that weary merrymakers could sit and have a coffee or a glass of wine. Paul, taking Lori's arm, gently guided her to one of these.

"I don't want it spoiled, Lori." His eyes were very dark, clouded with what could only have been worry. "You must listen to me very carefully; it isn't what you are thinking. It isn't . . . that I don't care about you."

"I know you care, Paul," she said, trying to sound easy, friendly, trying not to let her true feelings show. "We'll always be friends, I hope."

"Listen to me!" He leaned closer to her. Suddenly the noise, the happy shouts of the people in the streets, seemed to fade away. All she saw was his face, his dear, unhappy, beautiful face, so close to her own. "I cannot give what you must have, my little Yankee friend. What you must have, what you need, is a husband to love and to give you joy, and I cannot do that. Oh, I can make love to you, of course, and I daresay we would be quite successful at that. But that isn't what you really want or need, Lori. You need—"

Everything she had heard about this man was true, then. He was not interested in any kind of solid relationship. The sudden knowledge that under all her self-deception lay one blinding truth—she loved him—took over, and for a moment, all she could do was keep silent, while Paul ordered coffee, while just beyond them, people swarmed through the streets, praying, calling to each other.

"I want you to understand," he told her quietly. "I want you to know why I can't give you more than I have."

Lori managed a smile. "On the contrary," she said lightly. "You've given me some lovely tours of the city, some delicious foods that I'd never tasted before, those beautiful flowers——"

"Will you kindly stop that and look at me? Lori, look at me!"

She did, her eyes suddenly misting. "I'm trying," she said softly, "Paul, I'm trying very hard to understand you, I really am! All I know is—I'm trying not to respond to what you've said to me, what you apparently need from me and other women—the way I would have a few weeks ago. The world, such as it is, belongs to all of us. You can't regulate me to one small spot and tell me I must stay there until I die, because if I decide I want to live in your part of the world, it will somehow bother you." She took a shaking breath. "I came back here to Alexandria after making a decision, Paul. When I'd gone to the Valley of the Kings with the others, I thought about you nearly all the time."

"That was very sweet."

"Sweet? No; it wasn't that at all. Thinking about you didn't make me feel the way it should have, it made me feel a great kind of—*sorrow!*"

He shrugged. "I seem to do that to people. I find that no matter how hard I try, I end up making the woman unhappy."

Lori raised her eyes and looked at him. "Well, this is one woman you aren't going to do that to! I'm not going to let you destroy me," she said clearly, not giving him a chance to speak. "I'm not! I came back here quite determined to—to make love, to do anything I could to please you, to ease the hurt in you. I know about that agony because I went through it, too, Paul. You loved Betha; I loved Tommy. They both died, and they died in ways we would not have chosen for them; they died in ways that left us bitter and frustrated and enraged. I thought—I guess I thought that because I found I was able to love you, you would be ready

113

and able to love again, too." She picked up her purse. "Well maybe you are, but if you are, I guess I just don't happen to be the right girl for you!"

Suddenly she felt she had to get away from him. She did not want to cry in front of him; to cry would be demeaning somehow, a silly, feminine expression of disappointment.

"We must go someplace where it is quiet," he was saying, "Lori, you don't understand! It isn't that—"

He had reached for her arm, but she pulled away from him, standing up quickly, taking him by surprise. She turned from him, from the table and the noisy café, and ran down the street; she heard his voice calling her name but she didn't look back. At the corner of Tatwig, she darted through the procession of laughing, jostling people, cutting across the street, around a flower stand heavy with the perfume of flowers, and then she was somewhere on a dark and twisting street, not far from the sea wall and the sea beyond.

There she walked to the wall and stood looking at the dark, restless ocean. She had been wrong to think that by giving herself to Paul, by desperately trying to please and make him happy, she could ease his agony. She could not. Doubtless there had been many other women—Francine, the dancing girl called Jasmine—many others, all trying to help Paul Kardett.

And not one of them, herself included, had been able to dispel even for a little while, his burning memory of the girl who died while carrying his child.

She found an empty taxi parked near the mosque, with the driver happily sipping from a bottle of wine.

"Will you take me to the American hotel, please?"

He grinned, nodded, and started the old car. Lori leaned back against the seat, smiling if a smiling face peered at her from some doorway, or from the street. Some part of her hated to go back to the Teresa, to its somewhat cold lobby, its glass elevator, its luxury. She would like to have been able to join the procession, take hands with others and run through the streets like a happy child.

But she got out in front of the hotel, quickly paid the driver and hurried inside. The man behind the desk nodded as she came up to him.

"I'm Miss Coleman," she told him. "I'm not taking any calls tonight, if you please."

"Yes," she was told politely. "Very well."

She was halfway across the lobby when someone called her name—a male, almost unfamiliar-sounding voice.

"Aren't you Miss Coleman?" The tanned, narrow face of the man named Dobbie smiled down at her. "I've been hoping you'd come by. Been sitting in the bar watching for you as a matter of fact." His British accent reminded her of Julia's, when Julia was "putting on airs," as she called it. But with Dobbie the cultured accent seemed to be real.

"Hello," she told him. "I'm afraid I'm on my way to bed. I'm quite tired and I'd like to just get some rest. Enjoy your evening."

"I won't keep you long," he told her. His eyes were somehow anxious, and there was something, some kind of intensity, about his manner that kept her from going on, getting on the elevator. "Look, if you don't want a drink, we can order tea or something out here in the lobby. Just so I have a moment with you."

"I just had coffee," she told him. "Perhaps some other—"

"It's about Paul," he said quietly.

She followed him to a somewhat secluded area of the vast, polished, plush lobby—two armchairs placed in front of a brick fireplace, with potted plants all around them. There they sat facing each other; the tanned, well-dressed young man called Dobbie seemed somehow uncomfortable, but very charming and well-mannered.

"A sandwich perhaps? I'm afraid a lot of the hotel employees are out taking part in the celebration. Did you get to see any of the procession?"

"Yes, a part of it."

He looked at her. "But you came back very early."

Lori felt her face color. "Yes," she admitted. "I—I was tired. Mr. Dobbie, would you mind saying whatever it is you have to say? You tell me you want to speak to me about Paul; I have nothing to do with his life, so I'm afraid nothing you tell me about him can have much impact. I tried to—to help him, but I see now that he's beyond help. He doesn't seek it, doesn't want it."

Dobbie leaned back in his chair. He was dressed in a way that would have looked ridiculous back in the midwestern city where Lori lived and worked. He wore white trousers, white shoes, a blazer jacket with an emblem on it, and some sort of a little silken scarf tied around his neck. In spite of his Western, rich-man's clothes, however, there seemed to be some genuine feeling for Paul Kardett, some masculine friendship that had brought him here, had caused him to wait for her, so that he could speak to her about Paul.

"I can't help him," she said quietly. "I'm telling you I can't do anything for him."

"And what makes you think you should help him?"

"I . . . don't know. I guess it was all a mistake." She looked around her, feeling somehow uncomfortable. She had no intention of discussing her private feelings about Paul, not to anyone.

"Do you mind if I make a few sage remarks, my dear? I'd like you to know first of all that Paul Kardett is perhaps the most misunderstood man in this country. He is not

116

really welcome here and he is not really welcome in Jerusalem. Paul is not a political man; he cares nothing for the things of this world, even though he was born to them, handed great wealth." He leaned forward in his chair, reaching for a pipe. "Paul is a man of peace, a man who, if it hadn't been for the murder of his girl, would be totally happy today, I believe. He wanted to be married, to have children, to be a husband and father, and, I daresay, to take some interest in his father's fortune so that it wouldn't be lost for his own sons. Basically he is a simple man, a man with much love." He lit the pipe slowly, watching Lori over the match flame. "When Betha was murdered, it was a near deathblow for him. I say near, mind you. I've lived here, off and on, when I'm not in Paris or some other watering hole, for some ten years. I met Kardett shortly after the girl was killed. In fact I believe I was the only person he spoke to in any intimate way for years. When I'd go away, to get married or divorced or to gamble or to play polo or whatever, I'd always come back thinking he surely must have blown his brains out during my absence. I was always rather startled to find him still living."

"Please. I don't think I want to hear—"

He put out a thin hand to stay her. "But since you came, since he met you, I can tell you this, and I mean it: he's different. Oh, he mellowed during the years since it happened; he stopped behaving as if he's ready to wipe out Betha's family. But the consuming pain was still there, still buried in him, you see. About five years ago he began running, only he wouldn't call it that, I'm sure."

"Running?"

"To women. Then with women, and always, finally, away from them. They were his painkiller, or he wanted them to be. A few of them hung in there, stayed around. Francine is one of those."

117

"I'm really not interested in Paul's affairs," Lori said, getting up. "You don't seem to understand. Paul and I are—friends. I'm not even sure we're that, anymore."

"Don't leave him," Dobbie said suddenly, bluntly. "You've been the only person to be able to touch him, to touch his heart. I know him well enough to recognize the change that's come to him, even though he may not recognize it himself. If you leave him, he'll be doomed to the same stupid life-style I have, God forbid."

She was standing in front of the fireplace. "You don't seem to understand," she said softly. "He doesn't want me to stay." She turned to face him. "I was going to—to try to stay on, working at one of the hotels, here or in Tel Aviv, or perhaps in one of the other countries nearby. I told myself I wanted that because I love this part of the world, and I do—but that wasn't the only reason." She shook her head. "He was very upset about my wanting to stay. He told me . . . he so much as told me not to."

"Of course not. Paul doesn't want any sort of commitment, you see." He puffed furiously on his pipe. "But that doesn't mean you haven't been good for him."

"I'm not good for him," she said evenly. "I'm not good for him at all, because nothing has changed. He's still bitter and hurt and—alone."

"Not because he wants to be."

"I'm not so sure of that," Lori said quietly. "Good night, Mr. Dobbie."

"Just Dobbie, please. And may I see you again before you leave?"

"Maybe." She shook his hand briefly. "I've been no different for him than—than Francine or that girl who dances—"

"Jasmine."

"Good night," Lori said quickly. She certainly didn't

118

want to get into a running conversation naming off Paul's various women. Without another word she hurried across the quiet lobby to the glass elevators and pressed the button. When she got on, facing the lobby, Dobbie had gone, back inside the bar most likely.

Suppose, she thought, she asked Mr. Mulvaney to transfer her to say—this very hotel, working in the kitchen here instead of in the kitchen in the Chicago Teresa. What then?

Could she live here, find a life here, that didn't include Paul? Could she perhaps see him sometimes, see him with one of his beautiful women, and not suffer? She was, after all, weary of suffering, of feeling sorrow and pain, of not allowing herself to be happy.

She must. She vowed to speak to Michael Mulvaney the next day.

Eight

The surprising note from Francine came the following morning.

A fine morning it was, with dampness from the sea still in the air; the heat of the day had not yet begun. Lori was up early, out on the balcony brushing her hair when the discreet tap came at the bedroom door.

"I hope that isn't something to do with another blasted meeting," Julia said from her bed, where she'd been having early tea. "I'm meeting that crazy Link for breakfast." She opened the door, taking the note from the smiling Arab boy. "Lori, have you some American change?"

Lori tipped the boy and, wondering, opened the sealed envelope. It was very pretty paper, expensive-looking without being heavy. It was pale yellow and was written in a rather flourishing hand.

"Well, what is it, Luv?"

"It's an invitation, from Francine."

"Francine! What does that witch want with you?"

"She wants to take me to lunch," Lori told her, beginning to look through her closet. "At a place called Beaux Arts."

"Sounds very posh," Julia said suspiciously, "but then of course Francine wouldn't go to any other kind of place." She put down her cup. "The question is, what does she want?"

"To talk about Paul, I imagine." Lori suddenly gave up worrying about want to wear. She was rather sure that, no matter what, Francine would sneer at her outfit. Then why had she already decided to keep that unexpected appointment?

"See here," Julia said, horrified, "you aren't going, are you?"

"Of course." Lori pulled down a powder-blue skirt and a mauve-colored silk blouse she'd bought in Chicago, for the trip. It looked very American, somehow, compared to the lush things she'd bought here. It also looked rather—prim. "I want to tie up some ends, that's all."

"I'll never," Julia said, retreating back to her bed, putting the plum pillow over her face, "understand Americans!"

Lori couldn't help but smile. "Well," she said, "maybe you'd better try harder. And didn't you tell me you're meeting Link this morning. Get out of that bed, girl!"

"I really fail to see how you can take this lightly," Julia

told her, heading for the bathroom. "You know perfectly well that woman is going to give you a very hard time!"

"Maybe," Lori said, beginning to brush her hair with a harshness she usually didn't feel, "she ought to worry about *my* giving *her* a hard time!"

She walked part of the way to the Beaux Arts, taking a cab when she realized she would probably be late if she kept on walking. For some reason she wanted everything to be the way it should be. She wanted to let Francine know something she obviously didn't know, that even though she might never see Paul Kardett again, what they had was lasting and, in its way, very beautiful. She was not one of his "diversions."

And she didn't stop to ask herself why she felt she had to make this clear.

The large, very private restaurant was located on a winding side street, a tall, starkly white building with a large iron fence around it. There was a secluded, lush-looking garden in the back, so that the whole place seemed to be an expensive retreat from the pounding heat that rose up from the steamy streets.

It was comfortably air-conditioned, a place with linen tablecloths, thick carpets, and fresh flowers. Lori spotted Francine at once, sitting at a window table overlooking the garden. Probably the best table in the place. She walked toward Francine, who had waved in a cool, smiling way, but as she crossed that seemingly vast room, Lori suddenly felt very much like a schoolgirl, called to lunch with someone very powerful—and extremely chic.

Indeed Francine was that, sitting in her French crepe de chine dress, a sandy color that made her skin glow with its golden tan. She was attractive, but always, Lori had noticed, her eyes stayed cold, slightly narrowed, as if she was sizing up the situation.

"I took the liberty of ordering champagne," Francine said. "You do drink, don't you, Annie?"

"My name isn't Annie. It's Lori."

Francine smiled. "Of course. I knew it was something like that. Well, sit down and have a drink before we eat, darling." The eyes, those flat cold eyes, looked at Lori. "I can't imagine Paul having anything to do with anybody who doesn't love to drink. He adores parties, as I'm sure you know by now."

So this, Lori thought, was how it was going to be. A smiling mouth, furious eyes, and a voice that dripped with ill-concealed rancor. Well, it would be different this time, Lori told herself. This time it would be different from their encounter in the bathroom of the embassy, when Francine had been so vicious and she, Lori, had not been clever enough to put a stop to the nastiness. Now she felt she would be able to. For some reason she wanted this meeting to happen, if only, as Julia had said, because of her Irish background.

"I don't care for champagne to drink, thank you." Lori smiled politely, beginning to almost enjoy herself. "Mineral water would be fine, instead of the wine."

The arched, carefully plucked eyebrows went up. "Well, what a surprise! Or are you just playing Goodie Twos with me?"

Anger, quick, white-hot, rushed over Lori. Her hand trembled a bit as she raised the glass of sparkling water, brought seconds later, to her lips. But she managed to swallow it with the cool water.

"May I ask what the secret is, Francine?"

Francine was reading the menu, or pretending to. "Secret?"

"The real reason you asked me here, I mean. What is it?"

"Haven't you guessed?"

"Yes," Lori said, her voice low, guarded. "I imagine it's to warn me to stay away from Paul."

Francine, for an unguarded instant, looked startled. Then she looked again at the menu. "The crab salad is divine here, better than any I've had since Maxim's in Paris. I don't expect you've been there, have you?"

"I'm afraid not."

"Well, cheer up." She closed the menu. "Maybe you'll win next year's popularity contest and get to go."

"Mr. Mulvaney only lets us win once." *Easy*, Lori told herself. Can't you see this is what she wants, to get you all rattled and angry? For a moment Francine was silent. She ordered a salad and an ice fruit; Lori ordered only the fruit. She didn't see how she could manage to get down even that, with all the emotions churning around inside her as they were doing. Perhaps Julia was right; she may have been foolish to come here and expose herself to wrath and insults.

"Has he dropped you, Lori?" The question was abrupt and direct, totally unlike the clever Francine.

"How does one know if Paul has done that or not, Francine?" Lori looked at her adversary steadily. "Tell me what happens when he drops a woman. Does he stop calling? Does he stop sending flowers? Or does he simply forget to send messages around any longer?"

A slow, pink flush was coloring Francine's face. She was clearly surprised by Lori's retort.

"To be perfectly frank," Francine said finally, "I'll admit, I haven't heard from Paul in some time. But I've gone through that before, you see." She picked at her salad, and Lori suddenly realized that in spite of the cool manner, the

123

lovely clothes, and expensive perfume, Francine was a very worried person. Worried and probably miserable right now.

"And that's what you wanted to tell me? That Paul has had many women, that he's left them—but always comes back to you?"

"Yes," Francine said, after only a second's hesitation. "How did you know all of that?"

She hadn't known. Lori had taken a stab in the dark, so to speak, and she'd struck home. But the truth was she had dreaded to learn that Francine really did seem to mean something to Paul, that she was, in some mysterious way, important enough to him for him to keep going back to.

"I suppose there has to be some reason why you—" She had started to say *hang on to him so*, but out of kindness, she didn't. "—stay interested," she said finally. "I doubt if you would if there weren't some sort of relationship going on between the two of you."

"Of course we have a relationship," Francine said, beginning to gather together all her forces; clearly she still hoped to get Lori out of the picture. "We have had for years, in fact." Her eyes seemed to glitter with intensity. She was, a stunning young woman and probably would be even if she were not wearing expensive clothes, even if her short, shining hair had not been carefully coiffed. She was, Lori saw, a woman men were attracted to.

"Are you telling me I'm doing something to damage whatever it is you and Paul have together, Francine? Because that isn't why I see him."

"I'm telling you that you are nothing more than a simple diversion, that Paul has done this before and he will again, many times. The people we both know are different from . . . people like you." Her voice was oddly cool, even friendly as she said this. Lori realized with a mild shock that this beautiful woman actually believed she was not

124

only "different" from "ordinary" people—she was also far better. A special breed.

Lori put down her glass. "And how are we different, you and I?"

There was a small silence. A most imperceptible flush began to spread over Lori's face; she realized she was beginning to get angry with Francine. "Do you mean we're different because you have a lot of money and I don't? Or maybe it's because I work in a kitchen and you don't work at all." Cold rage began to fill her. She didn't really understand this sudden blinding anger that dried up her throat and mouth, making it strangely difficult to get her words out.

"I lost—someone who was very dear to me," she said, speaking low. "Did you ever go through that, Francine? Did you ever love a man and lose him to death, in a way that seems totally senseless to you? Well," she said, "I have. And if you haven't, then that makes us different, too."

"Look, there's no point in getting emotional about—"

"Emotional? No; I suppose not. Let's just be sure not to let any emotion, any human feelings, creep into what's happening here with us, Francine. Let's just keep things the way you want them to be: You're the more beautiful one, far prettier than I am, and you've much nicer clothes, and you're very clever and you're absolutely certain that one day Paul will marry you. You *are* sure of that, aren't you?"

"Well, I—yes," Francine said with some difficulty, "I am."

"So you'll finally be married to him. And you think you'll stay married to him because you're perfectly willing to allow him to cheat, to make love to any other woman he happens to see and like, am I right?"

"See here," Francine said, her eyes narrowing, "I don't

125

have to defend my relationship or my future plans concerning that relationship to you! Paul and I have been together for a long time, long before you came along! Let's get one thing straight—"

"Yes," Lori said quickly, quietly, "let's. Let's get it straight that the man you say you love and the man I care about are two different people. If he's really as you seem to think he is, I wouldn't want him. But thank God, he isn't."

The two women looked steadily at each other for a long heartbeat.

"You aren't what I thought as first," Francine said, and Lori felt she was being as honest as she could in that second. "I thought you'd be strictly kitchen door."

"I see. And I'm not?" Lori felt no hurt from Francine's attitude at all; in fact a small feeling of triumph was beginning to form in her. "You mean you thought I'd be more—"

"I thought you'd merely be a change for him, since you're American. I didn't, quite frankly, think you'd be a . . . formidable competitor."

Lori took a small breath. "I'm not, Francine. I'm really not. That's why I came here, you see, to get that clear, so that you'd understand once and for all. So that you wouldn't . . . talk about it as if it was something . . ." Lori raised her eyes to look at Francine . . . "usual."

"You mean it wasn't usual?"

"No," Lori said evenly, "it wasn't. It was very beautiful and we're good friends and I hope we always will be."

"Did you think I'd run about in the city and spread the word that you actually mean nothing to Paul?"

"Something like that, yes. And I guess I don't want it spoiled."

There, she said it, said she didn't want any gossip or lies or smut connected with the brief time she had known Paul.

She would, very likely, go home, at least there was a very good chance she would have to. And in no time at all everyone would have forgotten that the city's most infamous womanizer had once bewitched a young American girl for a brief spell.

Francine was lighting a cigarette. Everything about her, it seemed, had to be elegant, even her cigarettes. She drew one from a gold case, lit its pale pink tip, and exhaled.

"You're very much in the limelight just now, did you know that?" She smiled coolly, but only with her mouth; her eyes still watched Lori carefully, like, Lori thought, a hunter circling her prey. "Of course everyone talks of war here, but among . . . certain ones of us—"

"The elite, you mean?"

Francine shrugged. "Those of us who, shall we say, travel a good deal. Anyway my friends are placing bets on just how long Paul's latest fling will last. He's been known to drag out one of his diversions as long as two months." She blew smoke just over Lori's head. To Lori it carried a kind of stale aroma, Turkish and heavy. "Sometimes, however, the poor girl gets her heart broken much sooner than that." She leaned forward. "I know you're not a fool, you know. I didn't know it at first, but now I do. Surely you're smart enough to know that you're only asking for misery as far as your . . . friendship with Paul is concerned. Why shouldn't you enjoy your time here, see the sights, and when you go back, you'll have a lot of very pleasant memories?"

"I already have a lot of pleasant memories to take home with me."

Francine's eyes went totally cold. Suddenly she reached down and picked up her rather large hand-tooled purse. She took out a leatherbound checkbook.

"I'd like to do something to make your time here even

127

more pleasant and enjoyable," Francine was saying, not looking at Lori, busy with a slender gold pen, beginning to write a check with it. "The shopping can be divine, but very expensive. This way, you can—"

"Forget it, Francine; I don't want your money."

Her face very red, Francine slowly tore up the partially written check, dropping its pieces in the ashtray. "I still have an ace," she said finally. "I know his dark side—and I never try to change it."

"I understand that." There was a silence. "Thank you very much," Lori said, "for lunch. Good-bye, Francine."

And somehow, walking out of that quiet, plush, expensive place, she felt much better about things. It was almost as if she had protected something, or someone, very dear to her.

She was outside now, in the blazing heat; it came off the freshly water-slaked sidewalks and curled in little steam clouds around the stands that lined the street. Women sat in dark doorways, some of them nursing babies, some of them fanning themselves. A family sat on a corner, eating some kind of meat boiled in a cauldron that had been set right out on the street.

The hotel seemed very far away. Lori walked slowly through the crowds on the street, stopping only to buy a small glass of lukewarm tea, before walking on. Now some of the shop people seemed to know her; there was the beginning feeling inside her of knowing which stand had the nicest fruit, which place to stop and buy newspapers printed in English, where tea tasted the best.

The car, a rather small sports car, startled her when it pulled up beside her as she walked along. Paul was at the wheel.

"Hello," he said, and without another word, he held the car door open for her.

She hesitated only a second. Then she got in beside him, the little glass of tea still in her hand.

"I've been hoping for a taxi," she told him lightly, hiding the rush of sudden feelings that came to her. "Lucky for me you came along."

"You know," he said, skillfully maneuvering the car through the narrow street, going slowly, "I'm not going to take you to the hotel, so kindly stop telling me how much you hoped for a taxi. There's no reason for you to want to go back there, is there?"

"I'm not sure about staff meetings, and we're supposed to go to a dinner party at the American Embassy."

"What can they do to you if you don't show up?"

"Paul," she said quietly, "it's important that I know what the plans for the group are. It's also important that I speak with my boss about the job I'd like to have."

"So you still think you want to remain here?"

Lori settled back in the seat, determined not to let anything he might say hurt her feelings at this point.

"I wouldn't be the only American working for the hotel, you know. And since there's to be a new hotel going up in Tel Aviv . . ." She stopped talking, determined not to let the fact that he obviously didn't want her to stay around change her plans, if she could call them that.

"I followed you," he said quietly. "Does that make you angry?"

Did it? She leaned her head back on the soft green leather of that expensive Lamborghini. Suddenly it was very nice to know that her feelings for this man had nothing at all to do with his cars, his island, his never-ending supply of great material wealth. What was important to her was the look of his strong hands, the way his eyes darkened, changed color with his feelings, the fine stroke of his jawline. And even more than those physical things she felt

129

the strong, binding feeling between them, something neither had expected or perhaps even wanted. She was not, apparently, the kind of girl he usually sought out to ease his pain. He was not the kind of man she usually would like— he was too rich, too used to great wealth, too spoiled by women.

But in spite of all of this the feeling between them was there—strong, steady, seemingly growing and deepening.

She turned her head to look at him. "No," she told him, beginning to smile, "I don't mind."

"Good. I wanted to ask you to go with me to visit someone, but they told me at the hotel about your luncheon engagement with our friend Francine. So," he told her, turning onto the boulevard, going very fast, now that they had left the crowded, noisy side streets, "I decided to wait until it was over." He gave her a quick smile. "To tell you the truth I wasn't brave enough to get in the middle of it. I know Francine, how she can be. But I imagine you took good care of yourself." He seemed to be enjoying himself, she thought, as if it were some funny joke, having two women discussing him over lunch.

"I told her we're good friends," she said, staring straight ahead.

"Good. I'm sure she didn't believe you, however. You see, poor Francine is secretly hoping that one day I will marry her. She would never admit that is what she wants, but she does. Very clever, that one." He switched on the car radio. "But I am more clever."

"I'm afraid I'm not going to tell you what we said to each other," Lori said. "Even though I'm sure you want to know."

He looked at her quickly. "You're angry?"

"A little," she admitted. "I keep reminding myself that

you don't view women in the light that Western men do. At least not totally."

He was silent, and after a few moments Lori realized they had come to a side road that seemed to lead to a graveyard that held many tiny buildings, built in a huge circle around a mosque. Flowers grew wild everywhere, and on the slanting hill there were lemon and olive trees.

"Don't be frightened," Paul told her, bringing the car to a stop. "It's very peaceful here. Will you come with me?"

She got out of the car. Indeed it did seem to be peaceful here, with a moist breeze touching their faces as they walked.

"My relatives are buried here, some of them," he told her, taking her hand as they walked slowly around the winding, leaf-strewn pathway.

"Your parents, too?"

"No; they are in France, near Paris. I suppose my father knew there would be trouble, protests, if they were both buried here, and it would be the same if they tried to arrange burial near Jerusalem." He shrugged. "They had a villa there, so that is where I put them, near the house, in a country churchyard. They were Christians, you know. I daresay that didn't set well with their own families." He shrugged. "The point is they were very much in love. My father was a great romantic—he sent her a rose every day. He thought he would die first, you see, and she would go on getting the rose and she would feel so bad she would never remarry."

"I see. Wasn't that rather a dirty trick?"

"But she died first, you see." Paul sounded as if he were talking about old friends. "And *he* got a carnation every day, from her. She had arranged it before she died, long before, just in case. She knew him very well."

131

"And did it work, or did he remarry?"

"Remarry? After her? Never. Only," Paul said, "it didn't need the flowers or tricks of any kind by either of them. They believed they had been married before, you see. Perhaps several times."

They had stopped walking. He was staring ahead of them, and slowly he took his hand from Lori's.

"What you're telling me," Lori said quietly, "is that you believe in love. You learned that from them, of course."

He didn't look at her. "Yes. I do believe in love, very strongly."

Suddenly she realized what it was, why he had brought her here. For a blind second all Lori could feel was a kind of quick, blasting anger, to think he would bring her here, here to the heart, the core of his sorrow, and force her to share his agony with him, to watch him relive his loss.

"You had no right," she said suddenly, breaking away from him as he quickly reached for her. She turned and faced him on the pathway. "You might have asked," she said, her voice low. "You might have told me where it was you wanted to bring me!"

"Is it so unpleasant for you here?" He waved his hand around. "Look, there is so much fruit on that fig tree that it is bowed over. Is there something offensive about the richness of that? Or perhaps the grass here is too green, too soft for you to enjoy. Surely you know that here, no one will insult you or say anything out-of-the-way to you—"

"I don't find that very funny."

"And I don't understand your overreaction."

They faced each other. Suddenly Lori turned away from him. She hated arguments, bickering; long ago she had sworn to herself that she would never tolerate that in her life, not after her parents' endless, pointless arguments about everything they could find to argue about. It was a way of life with them, a kind of odd, friendly way of keeping life in their marriage. But she had hated it.

"I'm sorry," Lori said then, turning to look at him once again. "I just didn't plan to spend my afternoon at Betha's grave, that's all." She looked directly at him; her voice was low and steady. "I expect you spend a great deal of your time here, so if you don't mind, just drop me off and then you can come back here and mourn some more!" She began walking back toward where his car was parked. Her own words, spoken with such cool certainty, surprised her a bit. It wasn't like her to be this way, to demand her own way, to be downright rude, in fact.

But then he should have told her where he was taking her.

She suddenly realized he wasn't coming. Wasn't running after her down the hill, wasn't even calling out her name. And she realized something else, as she began to walk more slowly down the pathway, leaving the grove of olive and lemon and fig trees behind her: Betha wasn't someone to be jealous of; she was someone to wonder about. The fact that jealousy came into things at all was in itself shocking. Jealous—of a dead girl? A young girl who had loved Paul; that had been her only wrongdoing, to love him. For that they killed her and her baby.

Lori stopped walking. She stood for a moment with her head bowed, tears brimming in her eyes. Then she turned and, walking quickly down the path toward the trees, went back to where Paul stood alone.

The grave itself was somehow forbidding, a low, stone structure built like a cave into a swelling of the hill, similar to burial places used two thousand years ago. There was a little fence, with a picture of Betha tacked to it. The picture was framed and protected from rain, but as Lori stooped to see, she realized that already it seemed to be fading.

The girl in the photo seemed heartbreakingly young, but she was definitely a woman, petite and rounded; very beautiful, with shining black hair coiled around her head and braided. Her clothing was traditional, a long dress and sandals, but she wore no veils.

"She was lovely," Lori said softly. Gently she touched Paul's arm. "I'm sorry," she said then.

And she was; she was sorry for what had happened, that senseless brutal murder, the agony caused by it, the ruin of so many valuable lives because of the sadness and guilt Betha's death had brought. But now that was in the past and couldn't be changed. The lovely, shy, smiling girl in the photograph could not be brought back to the here and now; no human had the power to restore her, fill Paul's arms with her, let him see her smile or hear her laugh again. But Paul still walked this earth, and he needed human love, a woman's love, her kisses, her voice, her body close by his at night.

It was Paul, not Betha, Lori wept for. At the sudden, soft sound of her tears, Paul turned to her, surprised, and then he gently drew her into the strong circle of his arms.

"She would have liked you," he said against her ear. "She was very friendly with people, very sweet. She used to—"

Suddenly Lori pulled away. It was as if something, some muted anger, burst inside her and she wanted to strike him, shake him, do something to make him see what he was doing to his life.

"She's taking your manhood from you, Paul! Did you ever consider that?"

He looked stunned. "What?"

"Betha. Oh, I know how much she loved you—I understand that. I understand that because I'm unlucky enough to be in love with you, too!"

134

He took a step toward her. He had gone a bit pale under his tan.

"Lori—"

"I'm not begging," she told him, her voice trembling with emotion, "please don't misunderstand me, I'm not asking you to love me or even talk to me again. But whatever you do, Paul, give yourself to someone, love her, be happy with her, have children with her. Because one of these days you'll find that you're old and bitter and alone, and maybe then you'll realize that instead of worshiping at the altar of guilt, you could have been free and happy and you could have had a family!"

He caught her arm as she started to turn away. "Yes, guilt! Shall we speak of that, little one? Shall we speak of what happiness really consists of? Freedom, my dear, freedom from the horrors, the filth one has left behind." His eyes had deepened with feeling; they were dark, dark and luminous. "I killed her. I shouldn't have touched her, but I did; I made love to her and gave her a child and because of that—I killed her. That one truth eats at my spirit like a raw cancer, keeps me from all those good things you speak of. A man cannot take what he does not deserve." His hand left her. *"And I deserve nothing."*

It was as if he had left her, as if there were an ocean between them.

Lori realized she had given up hope for him. What kind of ego did she have, anyway, thinking she could change this man simply because she happened to love him? Why had she thought that a few choice, angry words from her could erase the agony he carried inside himself?

"Would you take me back to the hotel now, please?"

His eyes were grave and steady. "Of course."

So it was over for them. She felt exhausted, unable even

to hold up her head in the car. She leaned back against the smooth seat, closing her eyes.

In front of the hotel he put his hand on hers, but she quickly withdrew and without a word got out of his car and hurried quickly inside the Hotel Teresa.

Nine

The view from the room she shared with Julia was particularly lovely that late afternoon. The heat of the day came to a kind of dazzling crescendo about this time, so that, as Lori stood on the balcony facing the mosque across the street, she seemed to view it through a kind of misty, shimmering haze. Or that might have been only the unshed tears that kept flooding her eyes.

She knew she must get herself together, make her plans; if she really meant to stay here and work in either this hotel or the one across the border, then she must speak to Mr. Mulvaney, then tell Julia and the others she wouldn't be going back with them.

The sound startled her. She turned around and there was Julia, leaning against the bedroom door. Her blond hair looked rather wispy and for the first time since Lori had met her, she didn't look totally confident and able to cope. In fact she looked rather bewildered, standing there with her shoulders back, staring rather wild-eyed at Lori.

"Julia—what is it?" Lori went quickly to her. "Are you okay? Has something happened?"

Julia nodded silently, then went over and sat in the gold velvet chair by the window.

"What happened is that I think I'm going to marry Link."

"You, you don't mean you're—"

"Oh, no, Luv, nothing like that. Nothing quite that simple. What I'm saying is . . . that I'm in love with him and I'm going away with him."

Suddenly Lori ran to Julia and threw her arms around her. The solid, heavy feeling inside her, the sorrow-just-begun at losing Paul, lifted for an instant; she felt wonderful, wonderful, because of what had happened for Julia.

"Now you listen," Lori said, leading Julia over to the balcony. "You're always giving me advice, right?"

"Well—I guess I did—a few times—"

"And I always listened to whatever you said, about how I should wear certain shades of gold and green, and how I should wear my hair and lots of lovely little female tricks in order to keep a man going, as you put it." Lori smiled into Julia's worried eyes. "But now, I'm going to be the one to give advice, and I want you to listen to me. I know how you feel, how scared you must feel about embracing a totally new life, but here's something I'm sure of: If you don't, Julia, if you change your mind about Link and going with him, no matter if you're back in London Town or wherever, it won't be any good without him. That's the terror of it, you see—having to live one's entire life, no matter how long or short, without the somebody you love and need. Please," she said softly, "don't let that happen to you!"

"But I—I haven't told you where that idiot is taking me!" Julia looked as if she was about to break and cry. "*Alaska!*"

"You'll love it," Lori said firmly, "you'll learn to love it all, snowshoes, snowsleds, frosty nights—"

"And whale blubber, of course." Julia shook her head. "I know I'm going to feel rather like I'd stumbled onto some

137

strange, freezing planet that has nothing at all to do with me." She shook her head slowly. "The point is, however, I love the man and I want to be with him."

"Then be with him. And know how very blessed you are."

Suddenly Julia looked concerned. "You look terrible; what's wrong?"

"Nothing," Lori said, and then: "Everything. Paul—doesn't want me to stay around, that's all."

"I can't believe that. Not when he's been so attentive." Suddenly Julia began to look angry. "So that's it. He only wanted somebody to play games with, a kind of American diversion. I'd almost begun to think he wasn't any of the things I'd heard he was!"

"He isn't," Lori told her. "He isn't evil and he isn't out to buy women so that he can drop them and break their hearts, if that's what you mean. He's actually very wonderful, very good and kind—"

"Then why do you look as if you've just about given up and decided to be miserable?" Julia came over to Lori and looked at her. She was the taller one, making Lori suddenly feel as if she were back home, being gently scolded by one of her older, wiser sisters.

"I haven't done that. I haven't—given up on anything." She turned her face away, fighting tears. "Except Paul. I can't help him, Julia. I can't change his life, show him how easy it really is to love someone. I can't do that because he won't let anybody help him."

"I see. And where does that leave you?"

"Here," Lori said, "right here!"

Julia watched as Lori hurried about, throwing things into the suitcase she'd dragged down from the closet. "Lori, he hasn't decided yet, Mr. Mulvaney hasn't, about Paris,

138

about everybody's getting out of Alexandria and cutting short our time here. So there's no point in your packing."

"I'm going to visit a friend," Lori said firmly, checking her purse to be sure she had enough money left in American travelers' checks to pay for a round-trip ticket to Cairo and back. "At least I am if I can find her." She looked at Julia. "Is this good-bye for us?"

Julia's eyes looked stricken. "I never use that word. Never."

Lori realized that it was; it really was. "You'll be on your way before I get back then. Maybe I shouldn't go," she said. "But I thought, you remember that American doctor we met at the Valley of the Kings, Julia? She's stayed on here, made it her home, her world. She's left behind the life she knew before and she doesn't seem to miss it or have any regrets at all."

"All of which means you've made up your mind."

"No," Lori told her honestly. "I'm just not sure yet, that's all. And I don't think I should go back home feeling the way I do. I need to . . . get these feelings inside me resolved, and talking to Doctor Stephanie Palmer just might help me do it."

"Of course." Julia was suddenly very busy, packing. "Good girl, very smart thinking. Well," she said cheerfully, "since my Mad Yank is due to be on assignment at Point Barrow, Alaska, in only a few days, we'll be leaving as soon as he can arrange my passport business—changing my name and all of that. I'm not even sure where we'll be married. I'm trying to talk him into London, at the airport, if necessary. Nothing like telling one's great-grandchildren you married the old man at Heathrow, under the shadow of a 747!" She put out her hand. "So long, Lori."

"Promise we'll meet again sometime?"

"Promise. Now," Julia said thickly, "get out of here before I make a fool of myself!"

It was a quick flight that took Lori from Alexandria to Cairo, and once there nothing seemed to be different, not until she walked outside the air terminal into the bright hot sunlight, that is. Here things seemed to be very Western; people dressed fashionably in Western-style clothes, and with few exceptions, there were no women wearing the traditional long dresses and veils.

She felt a little foolish for having come, now that she was here. She might have been hasty in deciding to pay a call on a busy professional woman with whom she had actually had only a very brief and passing acquaintance.

Still, after a quick glass of spiced hot tea at the terminal, she found herself looking for the Good Shepherd Hospital in the phone book. Since it had burned down, she really didn't expect an answer, and the doctor herself wasn't listed in the book. For a blind moment Lori nearly gave up. She had a terrible urge to return to Alexandria as quickly as possible, so that she could spend a bit more time with Julia. But that, she knew, was being selfish; they'd said good-bye and, even though she hated good-byes, sometimes it was best not to go back and have to say them all over again.

The operator was, miraculously, ringing a number. Lori had briefly told her who it was she was looking for and now there was an instant, soft ringing in her ear.

"The Good Shepherd," an accented female voice said. "May we help?"

Lori leaned gratefully against the phone-booth wall, closing her eyes. "Yes, that is—I'd like to speak with a Doctor Palmer, if she's in."

There was an almost imperceptible pause. "May I ask who is calling, please?"

"Tell her it's Miss Lori Coleman, from Chicago. We met at—"

"One moment, please."

A buzzing in Lori's ear, then silence. She began to feel horribly embarrassed, as if she'd committed some unpardonable error by barging all the way over here, actually buying a plane ticket and coming all this way to—

"Yes," the pleasant, female, definitely Bostonian voice said, "this is Doctor Palmer."

"Oh, hello," Lorri said, flustered, "I—you probably don't remember me—"

"Of course I do, my dear. Are you in town?"

"Yes," Lori said, "as a matter of fact, I'm at the airport, and I, I was wondering if it might not be possible for me to speak with you. I won't take up much of your time, I promise."

"Are you ill?"

"Ill? No," Lori said quickly, "it's nothing like that."

There was a thoughtful pause. "I see," the older woman said finally. "Well, of course, of course. I'd be delighted to see you again! Why don't you get a cab and come over? We've had to move you know. We're on Little Flower Place now."

Lori felt an immediate sense of relief, a kind of certain, solid feeling that she had done the right thing. Somehow Stephanie Palmer reminded Lori of one of those choice, few, supremely good-natured and wise nuns one would meet from time to time during school days.

The city itself was sun-washed and seemingly much more modern than Alexandria, who, like an exotic old seductress, still had the throbbing mystery of a past that included such lovers as Cleopatra and the fiery, conquering Alexander himself. But here in Cairo one could step inside a fast-food, American-style hamburger place and have something

141

that, although it wasn't exactly McDonald's, wasn't too bad; they served sort of minced, highly spiced meatball, pressed into a bun that was hard but not stale-tasting.

It was in one of these places that Lori found herself, sitting across from Stephanie Palmer, thirty or so minutes later.

"I was starving for one of these," Stephanie said, smiling at Lori over the rim of a white coffee cup. "I'm not sure what triggered off my sudden yearning for a hamburger. Maybe because you come from home." She smiled, showing a dimple that was still that only, and had nothing at all to do with wrinkles. Those she had some of, however, gathered around her calm eyes like moored sailing boats, spanning outward, very attractive, really, in that tanned, intelligent face. "At any rate, you must stay over with me and have some very good Egyptian food. I've still got a sort of apartment at what is now our hospital, you see. We'll be getting funds for a new one before long, I imagine. But I'll miss my old quarters, at the old building." She looked at Lori. "How much longer do you have on your stay?"

"I'm not really sure. Our boss, the man who paid for the trip for all of us, hasn't decided yet when we're leaving. He's worried about the political situation, I suppose, or something like that." Lori felt much better, now that she was sitting here, in this strange, unfamiliar old city, with a woman she scarcely knew. But Stephanie held some sort of key, Lori felt, to a great secret. Once having it, it made one calm and sure and dedicated and—resigned to living whatever kind of life one was destined to lead, without trying to make it different or fighting it.

Lori felt that, sooner or later, Stephanie Palmer would tell how this had come about for her, and then, only then, Lori could make her decision.

Stephanie had brought her car, a small gray English

Ford, parked in front of the noisy, colorful place where they had gone to have the hamburgers, if indeed the meat had been beef, but Lori hadn't dared ask. Now Stephanie turned to look at Lori as they drove rather fast along a six-lane boulevard with stunning fountains in the center.

"So you aren't certain when your group is leaving?"

"No," Lori told her. "They'll be having a staff meeting to tell us, I imagine. If it's something that is going to happen at once, they'll call me." She was gazing out the window at the giant, sedate palm trees lining the avenue. "Even if they do," she said, her voice low, "I'm not sure if I'll go back."

"I see. And this is what you came for, to ask my advice?"

"Yes," Lori said, "this is why I came."

There was a silence. They drove off the main avenue, onto a quiet street with gardens and small, well-cared-for houses. It could easily have been a back road in any big southern city in the United States, with clothes gently swaying on lines, children playing in the shade, and pretty young mothers sitting about in front of their houses, talking, reading, some of them tending flower gardens that spanned some of the small homes from front to back.

"It's just over the hill," Stephanie told Lori, suddenly smiling. "The house where we've had to move our hospital. Actually it's my house; I bought it when I first came over here. I was going to pine away my years, you see." She was still smiling. Ahead of them there was a hand-painted sign that announced that this was the present site of the hospital but that they were not equipped to handle emergencies requiring certain things, all of which were put down in three languages. Stephanie drove slowly down the winding, narrow road, which led to a large house with a wraparound front porch and large, drooping trees.

"It's lovely," Lori said, and it was. She had expected

143

something closer to the busy city, white-washed and clinical.

"A new hospital would be lovelier," Stephanie said, parking her car in front. Almost at once a little dark-eyed girl wearing a nurse's uniform but no cap came out to greet them."

"Welcome home, Doctor."

"Thank you, Danya." She turned to Lori. "Danya studies nursing and helps us out here, too. We keep her very busy."

The girl smiled at Lori. "We all keep busy here."

How lovely, Lori thought suddenly, as she followed Stephanie Palmer down the hallway, to be so dedicated to a way of life, to feel in one's heart that whatever the choices had been, it was the right choice that had been made! She followed Stephanie to a screened-in, comfortable porch.

There seemed to be beds everywhere, even in the hallway, and in the large rooms that ran directly off the hallway, rooms that had very likely been the living room, a huge dining room, and probably a library. On the screened-in porch there were two patients chatting, both of them in wheelchairs.

"Sorry about those dreadful hamburgers," Stephanie said, smiling. "I promise you some lovely *malfoof* tomorrow—we've an excellent cook here, a fugitive, by the way, from the hotel business. We stole him from the Hilton in Tel Aviv. He's really amazing and loves to show off, providing you'll stay over. You will, won't you?"

"Yes," Lori said, "I'd like that very much."

"Would you prefer to talk now about whatever it is that brought you to see me, or would you rather wait awhile?"

"I may not have much time," Lori said, and she realized how important it was for her to talk to someone who would understand. "Anyway, there isn't much to tell you, really.

I—I'm thinking of staying on here, you see. Not in Alexandria perhaps, but at any rate, I'm not sure I want to go back home again."

"I see. And you must decide quickly, is that it?"

"I suppose so," Lori said. "Yes, fairly quickly, at any rate. Mr. Mulvaney might have already decided we're to go home again, right away. Or at least to Paris."

"Paris!" Stephanie smiled. "Now, my dear, if you're going to fall in love with a city, why not make it Paris? People back home might understand more easily, you know."

"Yes," Lori said, smiling. "I suppose my Aunt Edith would be more likely to give her blessings if she thought I'd taken an apartment near Notre-Dame than if she heard I'm living on a back street in Alexandria, near a mosque!"

Stephanie gave her a long look. "Well, then? What about Paris?"

"No, I couldn't. What I mean is—"

"You're in love with the city, is that it? Alexandria has completely captivated you, with its fish smells, its beggars and thieves—"

"It's much more than that," Lori said.

Stephanie nodded. "Yes; of course it is. But you haven't told me about the man. There is one, if I remember correctly."

"I'm going to make my decision without considering him," Lori said quickly, her face coloring. "I'm not basing anything that has to do with my future on—on the man. I mean, he doesn't, he isn't—"

"He doesn't want a complete involvement, is that it?"

"Yes," Lori said, letting her breath out. She turned her face away, feelings of misery beginning to form inside her. But she pushed them away: she was not going to let Paul Kardett ruin her life! "You see," she said carefully, "there

145

was someone else in his life, a girl who died. He prefers to live with her memory."

"Is that all? Are you perhaps being vain, my dear?"

"Do you mean vain because I insist on believing he actually loves me?" It was true; she did somehow believe that, at least most of the time she did. If it were not for his grief over Betha, he would love and accept her; she had wanted desperately to believe that, hadn't she?

"Suppose," Stephanie said, settling herself in a wicker rocker that afforded a sweeping view of the hills beyond, "you take a job in your beloved and mysterious city, and one fine day or night you run into your ex-true love with another girl. What then? Do you decide to run back to the States, or what?"

"I fully expect to see him with a lot of other women, from time to time." Lori's voice was steady. "In fact there are other women right now." She looked candidly at Stephanie. "You haven't asked his name."

"No; I haven't." Stephanie smiled. "But perhaps I will—later."

Stephanie had her living quarters there in the house; she had moved the patients in shortly after the fire, and now her own rooms were confined to a makeshift kitchen upstairs (the main, downstairs kitchen was used solely for cooking patients' meals), along with a sitting room and a small bedroom. Lori's things had been put in the bedroom, although she'd asked to be allowed to sleep on the couch.

"Of course you won't," Stephanie said, as they sat having supper on the screened-in porch. "I'm on call all night, anyhow. More coffee?"

"No thanks. Stephanie, it's very good of you to let me stay and to take time to talk to me."

"I told you, I love having another Yank under my roof."

146

They ate in a delighted way; the cook had gone all out to prepare some of the local dishes—a baked fish stuffed with rice and herbs; flat bread coated with a delicious sweet and sour sauce which was served in tiny dipping bowls, and a delicious blend of raw vegetables, all of which were grown in back of the house, Stephanie told Lori. Finally dessert was brought in, a light sweet, coated with honey and stuffed with almonds.

"Do you eat this way every day?"

"Not always. We're always thinking up treats for the patients, since nobody who comes here is terribly sick. Of course we have to be a bit careful; we've a small grant, but funds aren't unlimited."

"Doctor Palmer—Stephanie—was there anyone, perhaps a man, who more or less influenced you to come here and stay?" It was an abrupt, even rude question, but Lori felt she had to know, because of her own locked feelings concerning Paul.

"Oh, yes, in school there was. We were going to open a clinic for the poor, in some desperately horrible place. What happened was he ended up marrying the daughter of a very rich and successful plastic surgeon. He's in partnership with said surgeon now, in Los Angeles, I believe." She shrugged. "That made my coming here difficult, I suppose, but it wasn't the reason I chose Egypt. A woman who's been abandoned may have trouble keeping her sights straight, but she'll know she can go back if she wants to. You, on the other hand, are free to decide right away, unless, of course, you're basing your feelings about Alexandria on your hidden feelings for Paul Kardett."

Lori's heart seemed to stop for an instant. "How did you know who it is?"

"There was some talk in the group at the Valley of the Kings," Stephanie said. "I heard your name and his linked,

147

and of course I know of the man's background. His power and money have made him a legend around here." Her eyes were very blue and kind. "He is very much an Eastern man, Lori, in spite of his education. But I'm sure you already have discovered that."

"Yes," Lori admitted. "I didn't try to change that."

"I'm sure you didn't. Nobody changes that man, least of all women. He's very determinedly attached to his beautiful dead—what was her name?"

"Betha." Apparently the story of Paul's grieving was well known. "Stephanie, are you saying it isn't—real? That his feelings aren't—"

"Oh, he's suffering, all right. Who can say what makes one man bend over with guilt and another forget and go on with his life? I suppose one might conclude that having one woman the way he did, if he ever allows himself to love again, it will be . . . world-stopping."

World-stopping. Yes; it had been that. For a brief time she had actually felt that way, as if time, moments and hours, had slipped away and they were suspended on a trackless time schedule; she had even begun to get her days and nights mixed up.

"He won't allow himself to love again," Lori said quietly. "So for the moment I'd like not to think about Paul. It's my life I'm talking about, Stephanie—my life, and what I ought to do with it!"

Stephanie's eyes narrowed; suddenly she was looking at Lori in a totally new way.

"I've seen patients like you before, you know."

Lori's eyes widened. "Patients? But I'm not—"

"Ill? Perhaps not, but you must admit you seem to be under some sort of psychic spell. How is it possible that a very nice, middle-class girl from—"

"Chicago."

"Yes, Chicago. How is it possible that she never before sensed that there might be a hidden spirit inside of herself? 'The random spirit searches for home in the nearest heart, and once there, brings torture by remembering another life.' Do you study Sanskrit, my dear?"

"No," Lori said, "and I'm not under a spell, thank you. I'll admit that, that it might seem unusual for an American to feel that she is very comfortable, exceedingly comfortable, in a part of the world she knows little about, but—"

"You're talking to an American who feels exceedingly comfortable in this part of the world, Lori, one I still know very little about."

"Yes," Lori said softly, "yes, of course. So you can understand that it might be possible for me to have fallen in love with Alexandria as well as with a man who happens to live in Alexandria, part-time that is."

They had come to an easily arrived at point in their new friendship that allowed each of them to be completely honest. This surprised them both; neither of them had though of friendship as such happening so fast, but it did, and there they were, equals, in spite of one being older and a professional, in spite of it all.

Lori reminded herself that her grandmother had told her that friends were like rainbows; one never really knew what day one might suddenly appear, with a sort of glow that surrounds saints in old pictures.

Did Stephanie have a glow? She seemed to, sitting there in the fading light, a very kind, witty, dedicated lady, a lady definitely in love with the job she had and the place where she lived.

And oddly enough Doctor Stephanie Palmer had the look about her of someone who has lost a lover but is not bitter. Yes, Lori decided, there had to have been a special man in this woman's life.

149

It was dark, and Stephanie had been twice called to check on patients who had come in on emergencies in spite of the sign out front. But it had been nothing serious, thank God, Stephanie told Lori, because if it had been, they weren't equipped to handle it.

Now they sat comfortably side by side on the porch once again, this time with a spiced brandy in their hands.

"I'll be leaving in the morning," Lori said quietly. "Thank you for having me."

"Either I've helped you tremendously, in some secret, unknown way, or else you've decided I can't help you at all." Stephanie turned her head to look at Lori. "Otherwise you'd surely be staying longer. Okay, which is it?"

"I beg your pardon?"

"Lori," Stephanie stood up, suddenly looking stern and almost motherly, "I happen to know how your mind is working just now. I've been giving you feedback about how wonderful it is to be free, live where one wants to, forget about family and old, dear friends and—escape." She smiled; her voice was warm, good-natured, and it seemed to Lori that it had a sort of serenity in it. "It took me years to really adjust myself to this life-style," she told Lori. "Then once I thought I was adjusted, I began to be plagued with memories, and I very nearly went back to the States. But I knew if I did that, if I ever went home, I'd never be able to come back here. I knew what I'd do, most likely, I'd take up residence in a hospital near the one where my ex-fiancé did his surgery, or, God forbid, in the same hospital, and instead of doing something useful with my life, I'd end up bitter and mad at everybody, just because some conceited pup who was more interested in money than anything else decided to do me the favor of not marrying me! So finally I came to love it here, everything about it. Here a broken heart is regarded as a fact of life; nobody hides from sadness. In fact they believe it's all predestined, and in many ways that makes life a whole lot less complicated."

"If I believed that," Lori said, smiling, "I'd have to believe that there was some spiritual reason for my winning that yearly contest the hotel holds every year for employees, and I'd also have to believe that I was destined to come here and to meet certain people."

"Perhaps," Stephanie said, her eyes suddenly serious, "you were, my friend."

"I prefer to think my reasons for loving it here are on a much more realistic level, that they are a combination of my life back home, the freedom I've felt since I came to Alexandria, and the city herself. . . ."

"You always," Stephanie said, "seem to get back to that, to Alexandria."

Lori smiled. "I'm in love with the city, at least I think that's it. Anyway I feel quite comfortable there, and the real reason I came was to ask you to help me—and you have."

"I can't see how."

"You're so . . . contented," Lori said softly. "This is your home, and you feel as if you belong here. I believe I've that feeling inside me, too. You see," she said, "if you can be happy here, so can I."

"Perhaps. But what about Paul?"

"I believe I can be happy here, with or without him."

"Well, my fellow American, I just hope you aren't kidding yourself. Because it isn't always easy, you know. Sights, sounds, even voices come back to one at times and you long for the way it was; you want to go back. I did that once, went back to Barnstable and walked down the street where Dad's office was, and where we lived, in the back. We'd sold it, took a loss on it, just to get out. But when I saw it again, some very rich people had bought it, and there it was, all dolled up and looking great, looking as if my father and my family and I had never even lived there. So it was easy for me to come here and stay here, Lori. I knew my past life was gone, whether I liked it or not. Do you see what I mean? You've a life back there! And a life consists of people; it's exactly that, people who make the memories that come back to haunt you."

"You don't look very haunted to me," Lori said, smiling.

"I'm not. But I've a feeling, my dear, that you would be if you simply did not get on that plane with the rest of your hotel people and go back home." Her voice had taken on a somewhat surprising tone of earnestness. "Love what you've felt here—both for the man and for the city. Take it with you and cherish it and keep it, but don't try to go on living it, Lori, because it wouldn't work. At least not in Alexandria, and I doubt if it would work in Tel Aviv, because in a sense it's tied up in Paul."

"I haven't the faintest idea of what you're telling me," Lori said, but some warning had sounded, something that told her she wasn't hearing what she wanted to hear, what she thought she had heard. "Are you telling me I ought to go on back home for good and forget my wild idea about staying on here, getting a transfer, a job, here? I'd be able to make a very nice living, thank you, and I could probably live at the hotel, in one of the smaller rooms. A lot of the American or French or British employees do that, if they want to. What I'm saying is, Stephanie, I'd be fine."

"And what I'm saying is that you're now talking to me as if I were your mother, and I'm not, remember?"

"I'm sorry. I guess I was doing that and didn't realize it." Lori realized she felt uneasy, as if something vital and worth fighting for was being questioned, pulled away from her, however gently. The point was, Stephanie was telling her to go on home.

"Okay, then. You see, my friend, the problem is you aren't admitting how you feel about Paul. Alexandria is full of Paul for you—memories must abound for you whenever you walk outside the hotel. You could live on those for years, I expect. And in the meantime, my dear, life would pass you by. It has a way of doing that to some people, you know."

Suddenly Lori felt beaten, worn out from the mental struggle. She had come here almost certain that Stephanie would tell her yes, of course, stay, stay and build a life here. But she had not done that.

Ten

At six the following morning Lori was brought early tea by a fat lady who wobbled as she walked to draw the curtains. Instantly the morning showed itself, clear, with a cloudless sky.

In Alexandria now, on the streets, they would be already doing business, selling coffee and bread and cheese and fruit to people on their way to work. It was always exciting to watch, like the beginning of a concerto that will rise to a glorious crescendo. Odd, she thought, to miss it so soon!

"You ought to stay the week," Stephanie told her downstairs, bringing her still another cup of tea. "I could use another aide around the place, believe me. Have you ever thought about nursing, or at least helping out, cheering people up, writing letters for them, things like that? You're a very decent and kind girl, Lori, I expect that's what attracted a man like Paul Kardett to you in the first place."

It was odd, the way people, even Stephanie, who at worst was probably twice as intelligent as most people walking around, always seemed to think she was some sort of girl scout, decent and kind. Add to that loyal, brave, and true and what came up was a rather round-faced Irish girl with fair skin, her share of the obligatory freckles, and straight white teeth, thanks to braces paid for by her rich Uncle Michael who lived in a big house and who owned a big Irish tavern over on the south side.

But it wasn't herself, not really, not at all. She just seemed to come out that way, with most people, even this good and wise woman who had told her what she hadn't wanted to hear at all: *Go home.*

"If I stay, they'll leave without me, probably," Lori said, and suddenly, she felt very ready to leave, almost in a hurry to leave the tranquility of this place, even the good company of her friend, and go back once more to the city she felt a part of. There was probably very little time left and she wanted to walk one more time down the now-familiar twisted streets. "But I promise I'll do a lot of thinking when I get home, about a lot of things."

"Then you're going, you're definitely going?"

Lori smiled, holding out her hand. "Yes. But not for the reasons you think, you see. Not because I'm a hopeless, silly girl who came here and has had a very nice time and who thinks she wants to stay on because it's going to be a holiday forever. It isn't like that at all, you see. The truth is, I'm very much like you. I could live here and work here and be happy here in this part of the world, just as you are. I might even take you up on your offer, except for one thing: I've got a family back home and they wouldn't understand. It comes down to that, I've an obligation to them, to all of them. It would be like—running away from that."

"You've no obligation to live a life-style that isn't right

154

for you," Stephanie said firmly. "but on the other hand, I'm not so sure that your feelings for the man in this case haven't tinted your ideas about Alexandria. I find the place unbelievably dirty, vicious to a point of being actually dangerous, and, when the wind goes right, extremely smelly. I can't imagine why you'd want to move there." Suddenly she grinned. "But then nobody back in Boston could understand why I wanted to move to *Egypt!*"

Riding toward the airport, to get the flight back to Alexandria, Lori sat quietly in the back. It was amazing, the way she had been able to make friends since coming here. Back home she had been a pleasant-natured but basically solitary girl, at least since Tommy's death. She had never taken to her bed, as they said, after his death; the women in her family had not been schooled to do that sort of thing. They were taught to be strong in the face of adversity. So she had managed never to cry, always to be pleasant, and to hide the bevy of real feelings inside her, where they remained unresolved, until finally, finally, she had gotten away from the places that shouted to her about Tommy. . . .

She dozed on the plane, surprised at herself when she woke up. The gentleman sitting next to her was from Saudi Arabia and he kept brushing her finger with his hand. Oddly enough it made her laugh and suddenly things seemed a whole lot better, because the man, turban and all, grinned like a naughty boy caught at doing something he shouldn't, and from then on they were comfortable, sitting silently side by side. But at the airport he remained at her side.

"There you are," a voice said suddenly, and she whirled around.

"Paul!"

He glared at the man in the turban, who shrugged and walked away.

"Who the devil is that?"

"Never mind. What's happened? You look—" Dear, she thought. Very dear to me. You're giving me another memory to store away, just by being here.

"I've gotten word that your whole group is leaving. They've been looking for you, sending cables and messages—"

"But Julia knew where I was! I told her; she could have had them call!" He had whisked her across the wide, busy terminal, through an exit door and out into the hot sunshine. She looked up at him; he needed a shave and he looked rather rumpled and weary.

"The car is around the corner. Here," he said, "give me your hand." Then he put her hand quickly to his lips. "I was afraid I'd never see you again. I've been up all night looking for you."

"But, I can't believe that she—that Julia wouldn't tell people where I was! Unless she's gone, unless she and Link have gone—"

"No; at least I don't think so. I spoke to her last night about you, at the hotel." He made a signal and in seconds, the Rolls descended on them, with the driver hopping out to assist Lori in getting in. Paul slid in beside her and immediately leaned forward, shutting the connecting glass. Then he turned to her. "You can't go back with them, you know. That's why I had to see you again, so that I could talk to you about that."

She had a sudden soaring sensation inside her, as if great joy had come, come like a dove flying in an open window, startling one and yet, so lovely that it was breathtaking. The thought danced into her mind like notes of music: He wants to marry me!

156

"I walked about all night, like a madman," he told her, reaching into a liquor cabinet on one side of the car. "I thought about kidnapping that woman, Julia, and forcing her to tell me. But I didn't. She's really a very lovely person, although I didn't believe a word she said."

"And what did she say?"

"Oh, a lot of hogwash about your having left suddenly for Paris. I knew she was lying. I knew you'd stay on as long as you could, or at least I thought you would. Champagne?"

"No thank you. Paul, I'm not sure what it is you're saying!"

"Then let me say it clearly." He suddenly drew her to him. "But first, we have to stop Mulvaney from leaving." He tilted her face upward and bent his head; his mouth was warm and probing. She felt lost, lost in that kiss, and as always had to push herself back to reality, back into the world.

"Why is it whenever you should be explaining something to me, instead you kiss me?" It was true; he seemed to sometimes kiss her instead of talk to her. She still had that dim feeling, like a nagging sore, that something was terribly wrong between them. At first, moments before, when she had first turned and saw him there, she had felt such happiness that she'd been giddy, lightheaded, unable to think straight. But now, in just a short time, she found herself beginning to feel uneasy, as if she must beware of something, hold something of herself back, or else she'd be lost, lost—

"Give me the proper time and place," he told her lightly, refilling his glass, "and I'll explain it very fully and very clearly. But as I said, first I must talk to your employer and convince him to hold off on his sudden rush to take everybody to Paris. Paris is very dull this time of year, you know."

"No," she said, still with that feeling of uneasiness, "I don't know."

He held her gently against him on the ride back to town. In the hotel he kissed her hand, bowed gallantly, and more or less ordered her to meet him in the cocktail lounge in six hours. In the meantime he would be talking to Michael Mulvaney.

Lori, feeling somewhat baffled and windswept, found herself saying a small, pleading prayer that Julia hadn't left yet, that she was still there in the room, messy and clever and mad at herself for having fallen in love with a man she considered not to be what she wanted at all.

"Julia? Julia, are you here? *Julia!*"

The door to the bathroom was closed; Lori knew at once that she was too late; Julia was gone. But her perfume lingered, and inside the bathroom it was still steamy. Lori pushed open the window and then turned to find a scrawled message written in eye pencil on the mirror; "Okay, Yank, go ahead and be mad at me—I didn't tell him where you were because I don't want you hurt. If you ever get to Point Barrow, Alaska, look up my igloo. Luv, J."

Too late. Too late to talk to Julia about anything now, and too late to stop the sudden switch in events that had suddenly brought Paul into her life again. Maybe it wasn't over after all. Maybe she wasn't going to have to go back home like a dutiful little girl; if there was one reason, one thing her family would understand, it was marriage. If she were married, she could live on Mars, and as long as she came home for Christmas, that would be fine with them. They would accept and approve of marriage for her, but as for her working so far from home, as a single girl—never.

She didn't unpack, thinking Paul might phone her, but

he didn't. He must have ordered lunch for her, however, because it came on a tea cart, with a single rose in a silver vase, next to various covered dishes; all of them looked delicious.

Did he really expect her to sit in her room all day, waiting for him to tell her what was going on? The more she thought about that, the more the warning in her got louder, until finally she took a quick bath, put on flat-heeled walking shoes and a comfortable cotton dress, and was halfway out the door when the phone rang.

"Lori? This is Frank Corita. We're having an emergency staff meeting at once in the garden."

"Has something happened?"

"You'll find out when the others do. Just be there."

"Yes, Mr. Corita."

The room seemed horribly lonely without Julia; Lori found herself reading the eye pencil warning on the mirror over and over. Then she picked up her purse and, ignoring the lunch on the cart, went down to the east garden, where Frank Corita and the other managers and staff had gathered, sitting on stone benches or on the soft, nurtured grass.

"May I have your attention, please, ladies and gentlemen?" Frank put up a pudgy hand. "As you all know, Mr. Mulvaney has decided to cut short our trip here and give you all the additional treat of Paris. There you will stay on the Right Bank at our beautiful Parisian Hotel Teresa, and you will be given various sight-seeing passes. However—"

There was general clapping and hooting, signifying that nearly everybody was more than ready to leave Alexandria and go to Paris. In the background Lori sat alone on the grass, silent and listening. Her mind seemed to be somewhere in Limbo. A part of it told her Paul was trouble, that there was something deeply wrong with their relation-

159

ship, with him, perhaps with her for having fallen in love with him. But a part of her yearned to have him ask her to stay, want her to stay with him. Loving a man, to Lori, had always meant wanting to be his wife.

"—slight delay," Frank was saying, "due to the generous invitation of a gentleman named Kardett, we are invited to a party on his island, so therefore we will be leaving for Paris tomorrow instead of tonight, as originally planned. Kindly gather in the lobby at six this evening, so that we may all be afforded transportation to the island." He wiped his brow with a clean handkerchief, looking for all the world as if he only wanted to be back in Chicago, which was true. "Until then," he said, and he headed for the downstairs bar.

For the rest of the day, until time to meet Paul in the lounge, Lori walked. She still felt suspended, not knowing if she was going home or staying—with Paul. The happy thought kept spinning around in her head, but it seemed somehow out of reach, as if she dared not really examine it. For this one day she vowed she would be happy. If this was to be her last day in Alexandria, it would be a happy day.

And it was. She stopped at open stands and bought things, inexpensive things that enchanted her: a tiny, carved statue; sun-warmed oranges; a little hand-woven shawl, light and the color of new grass. It would bring out the green of her eyes, perhaps cause them to look emerald-colored. She realized, walking down the narrow streets, where people pushed along, sat in doorways staring, drove by in expensive French and American and British cars, or leaned out of windows calling out things she didn't understand, that she could walk these streets for the rest of her life and gain the very same pleasure she felt now. Yes; Paul was there, and she would be seeing him soon; she had at least another twenty-four hours to count on. He had seen to that—he'd very likely come upon the idea of having the party at the last moment, and, that being so, he must have done it to keep her with him a bit longer.

She suddenly felt her heart catch as she bent over some silken material. If he would do that, go to all that trouble just to keep me here another day, then whatever he wants to talk to me about must be something terribly vital and terribly important!

But if that were so, why was he setting the stage, going to all this trouble? If it really was marriage he wanted to discuss, why hadn't he just come right out and asked her? Why the delay?

It was getting late. She finally took a taxi back to the hotel; the lobby was empty except for a small group of reporters gathered in one of the small downstairs bars. They were singing out of key and trying to get New York on a somewhat tinny-sounding shortwave radio.

She was nearly to the elevator when someone called her name.

"Dobbie!"

"Yes," he said, grinning, his face slightly red, "It's me—the bad penny. Actually I've been watching for you."

Lori put out her hand. "I've been saying good-bye to people since yesterday."

"Does that mean you've decided to go home?"

She began to feel uneasy. "Yes. That is, I talked to an American friend of mine, a doctor, and she thinks it best."

"But you aren't sure, are you? Paul has made you have second thoughts."

"I love it here, if that's what you mean."

"Love? One doesn't love a miserable, thieving, disgruntled city like this one, my dear. One only learns to understand her, and after that, a certain fascination sets in, the way we keep on admiring aged actresses who somehow

161

manage to always look the same to us." He took her arm. "May I speak with you a moment? It's terribly important."

"Dobbie, I have to dress, there's to be a party—"

"I heard about it. I'm invited, too, naturally. I think he had his people get hold of everybody in the city, including all the Embassy people." He looked at her. She saw that his pale eyes were worried. "How does it feel to know he did all of that—for you?"

Her face colored. "Wonderful, of course."

"How about a drink, Lori? We needn't go in there. We can sit in the garden instead of the bar, if you like. I'm sure men would swoop down on you if I took you to anyplace where they are. And I must have a word with you—about Paul. About you and Paul."

Instantly she was wary. "Dobbie, I'm not interested in discussing—"

He took her hand, very suddenly and firmly. Then before she could protest, he was leading her to the glass doors that fronted the garden.

"Now," he told her, "sit over there like a good little girl and listen very carefully to what I'm going to say to you. When I spoke to you before, Lori, when I talked about Paul, I didn't really expect things to go this far between you."

"Things haven't—"

"Oh, yes they have, my dear, only you don't fully understand just what it all means quite yet. While you've been taking your walk, things have been happening here at the hotel!"

She found herself believing him all of a sudden. Maybe he drank too much and was far too involved in other people's lives, but she had the clear feeling that he was basically decent and that he cared about what happened to her.

162

She remembered what her grandmother had said about friends popping up in strange places.

"What sort of things?"

"Sit down," he told her, indicating two yellow chairs near one of the fountains. He was silent, though, even after they'd settled themselves in the chairs. "Now, I don't want you to start crying on me, or anything ridiculous like that," he told her.

She'd been thinking of what to wear, whether to wear one of the gorgeous, sensuous dresses she'd bought over here or whether to wear one of the pretty dresses she'd bought in Chicago. Suddenly none of that was important.

"What do you have to say to me that would make me cry?" Her heart had begun beating faster, but her voice sounded very light and casual. "Really, Dobbie, I can't spend time on dramatics. See you at the party, and better stay out of the bar until then or you won't even make the party!"

"Dammit," he said, and he sounded actually desperate, "you've got to listen to what I have to say! You don't want to listen, do you?"

She was silent for a few heartbeats. "All right," she said finally, her chin rising, "maybe I don't, Dobbie. Maybe I don't want to listen to you tell me that it's all wrong, all some kind of, of a joke, that he doesn't really care about me at all."

"He *can't* care, don't you see? He can't because he won't allow himself to! And all the rest of it, all the gifts and the money and the show and the promises are because he has to cover up the fact that what women really want from him, beyond sex and beyond his power and his money, he can't give them."

"Are you saying he can never give love?"

"Exactly." He motioned for an Arab boy to come over

163

to them. "I only wanted you to understand what it's all about. It's part of a kind of ritual with him. He goes through it when he meets a woman who really fascinates him."

"Like Francine?"

"Once, Francine, yes. I doubt if he's seen her at all lately, not since he ran into you, that is." He glanced at the boy. "Whisky and soda, please. Might as well get properly drunk, since it's going to end up being such a sad occasion."

"Nothing for me; I'm going to dress." She smiled at him. "I'm just not going to let you or anybody spoil it for me. I want tonight to be perfect!"

"Why? So you can feel rotten about it some future time? Do you think everything he gives a woman is really worth—"

But she didn't stay to listen. Dobbie, she told herself, once up on the floor where her room was, drank too much; was too preoccupied with the lives of others; had no life of his own, poor man; had too much money and too much time to do nothing but sit around in expensive bars worrying about his rich friends and complain about how awful life was.

She had no time for that kind of thinking!

She found her room key in the bottom of her purse, underneath the things she had bought at the street market. She let herself in; the drapes had been drawn, for some reason, and the room was dark and shadowy.

At first she thought someone was there, standing in the shadows, near the bathroom. Then her fingers, trembling, found the light switch and she saw that it was not a person but a very large pot with a fig tree in it that had been placed by the bathroom door. Beyond that, crowding into the bathroom, filling, in fact, nearly every square inch of

164

space, were flowers, and fruit in baskets, and hanging on a chair a pale-green satin robe, with fuffly slippers placed carefully beneath it. Dazed, Lori wandered among the flowers, far more than there had been the first time he sent them, when she and Julia had gotten such a kick out of them, finding, as she walked about the room, one present after another: a pretty pair of slippers, white soft leather with high, graceful heels and a name that came from Paris inside them; perfume, at least three bottles of it, tucked under pillows on the couch, one on the dressing table; alongside it a beautiful, filmy shawl, of the most exquisite material she had ever seen—a rainbow of delicate shades of pastel green. She put it impulsively around her shoulders and turned this way and that, looking at herself in the triple mirror over the dressing table. Her face was pink with excitement and her eyes glowed green, catching the colors of the shawl.

She went over to the bed then, shoving bouquets of long-stemmed roses, pink and peach, gently to one side. There was a small, square box on the pillow, with some sort of note tucked in it's wrapping. It had been beautifully, expertly wrapped, foil paper drawn up in such a way as to resemble an opening rose. Who, she wondered, had done all of this, arranged all of this? She was certain it was Paul, at least he had paid for it, but to be able to *do* it, get it all done, order people to order flowers, to pick out jewelry, and send someone around later to pay for it, and on top of that, tell other people to arrange for the party that was fast becoming the talk of social-minded Alexandria . . .

That took power. And money—precisely what Dobbie had been trying to say to her. Paul had plenty of that, more than his fair share, in fact, more money than he could ever spend, even with his deeply extravagant habits. It was as if, in buying things for people, looking after people, like the street children, for instance, he could somehow atone for a grievous sin.

Her fingers trembled as she undid the satin ribbon. She carefully peeled the foil paper away and lifted the tiny lid, peeking inside.

The stone was stunning in its brilliant, glowing greenness, and it seemed to be perfectly cut. It was huge, glowing like a lovely cat's eye.

She put the box down, not touching the ring, slowly opening the sealed envelope with the note from Paul: "This was my mother's ring. There will be flowers every day of your life if you will only stay here with me. P.K." And another note, pinned to the satin robe, that read: "Don't go, little Yank. P.K."

She went into the bathroom, where flowers nearly hid Julia's cryptic message on the mirror. All of this, every single day of her life? He would buy her things and smile into her eyes and make passionate, sweet love to her. He would fill her life with himself, and she would love him with a singleminded purpose, which was the way he wanted it.

What, if anything, was wrong with any of that?

Suddenly she jerked the shawl from her shoulders and shut the door, turning on the hot water in the shower. At least there were no flowers in there. She undressed, then stood under the warming water with her eyes shut. Once she thought she heard a sound, coming from the bedroom.

Finally she shut off the water, reached for her robe and, belting it, pushed open the bathroom door.

Julia was calmly sitting cross-legged on her bed, having opened one of the boxes of candy sent along with all the other gifts.

"Julia! Where—"

"Where'd I pop in from? The airport, my pet. Link's gone on to Alaska." She tasted a piece of the candy, then pinched another and tasted that, putting them both back in their delicate little papers. "I'm looking for mint, cream mint, it is, and my second choice is strawberry."

"Julia, I can't believe you've come back!"

"Of course I have," Julia said calmly. "There's the mint; now all I have to do is find a strawberry."

"Will you kindly stop eating long enough to explain something to me?"

Julia had popped a piece into her mouth. "Explain what?"

"You and Link, you said he went on without you."

"He's stopping off in London to visit my mum and dad. I doubt if they'll like him, though. If it couldn't be royalty or somebody as rich as Mr. Paul Kardett, they'd much prefer I settled down in the mews with a nice chap who works at the foundry. That way they'd get to see the grandchildren more often. And I can't blame them, really." She looked at Lori. "Loving shouldn't hurt, should it? I mean it should be all warming, good, like wine that tastes marvelous."

Lori sat on the edge of the bed. "I'm delighted to see you; I suppose you know that."

Julia grinned. "Link and I heard there was going to be a party before we took off for Cairo. I told him I couldn't very well miss the poshest party of my life, especially since I'd be spending the winter unfreezing my eyelashes. He was very understanding. We're going to meet in London, day after tomorrow."

Neither of them said so, but they both knew the real reason Julia had come back was to try to save Lori from something. *But what?*

Eleven

By all that was right, it should have been the happiest night of her life. Lori kept telling herself this as she dressed for the party. For one thing the thought of what had finally happened to her made her feel a bit giddy, so that everything seemed to take on a dreamlike feeling, as if it were all actually happening to someone else.

Even Julia felt that way as she straightened her hose and peered critically at herself in the mirror.

"You couldn't look prettier," Lori told her. "Now stop worrying."

"I'm not worrying about that," Julia said. "It's you, Luv, what's about to happen to you."

"Julia, the only thing that's about to happen to me is that I'm going to be happier than I've ever been in my life—just as you are. It's going to be perfect, don't you see?"

"Nothing," Julia said dryly, "is perfect. Oh, by the way, you had a call from Cairo. Your American doctor friend, I expect."

"Stephanie called here?" Lori, who had decided to wear a simple, floor-length dress she'd bought on sale in Chicago, put down her hairbrush. She looked flushed, feverish, and as she picked up the phone, her hand trembled a bit.

The switchboard operator down in the lobby confirmed that there had been a call, and if she would just hold on, it would be put through for her, since the doctor had left a number.

Stephanie came on then, her voice cheerful.

"Back safely, I see. I'm glad I caught you before you left for home, Lori."

"Stephanie, is something wrong there?"

"A woman just had a baby on my living room couch; other than that, we're still fine here. I called because I wanted to tell you I've been thinking a lot about our last conversation, the one where I practically kicked your behind back to the States."

"That's okay. Maybe I needed a good, swift kick."

"That's just the point, honey—you didn't. I really think you've a feeling for this part of the world, maybe rusty hills and hot sun looks beautiful to you, just as it does to a lot of us. Anyway if you ever decide to come back, you've got a job waiting for you here, with us."

Lori closed her eyes, because in that moment she was feeling wonderful; if Stephanie Palmer felt she ought to stay, then her own feelings made sense, even more sense than before.

"I'd never noticed that they're the color of rust," she said. "I'll have to make a note of that."

"See you, Lori."

"Sure. And thanks."

Julia came up from behind, carrying Lori's little evening jacket.

"Come on, Luvvie. Time to go to the big bash."

Lori had not, for some reason, mentioned Paul. She had not told her friend Stephanie that she might well be staying on here, but that, as Paul's wife, she would be expected to do other things besides work in a faraway city in a makeshift hospital.

She looked into Julia's blue eyes as she put on the jacket. There was worry in them, obvious by their starkness.

A knock on their door startled both girls. "If it's more

flowers," Julia said, "I'm going to start tossing them down the elevator shaft!"

It was Michael Mulvaney himself, wearing a formal tux, looking a bit flustered and excited.

"Ladies," he said quickly, "we can't be late tonight!"

"We have no intention of being late, Mr. Mulvaney." Julia's voice was poised. "We'll be down in five minutes."

"That won't do, ladies. As a matter of fact the press wanted an interview ten minutes ago, with Miss Coleman."

Lori felt her eyes widen. "The newspaper people want an interview with me? But I've nothing to say to them!"

"I'll handle it," Julia said grimly. "Link gave me all sorts of advice on how to sneak away from people one doesn't want to bother with. He's an expert at it, believe me. See how smoothly he managed to get to London, while the rest of us are still stuck here?"

"Stuck," Mr. Mulvaney said, almost whispering, "is a word we never use in connection with anyplace there happens to be a Hotel Teresa!" He glared at Julia. "The plan is we will all three go down together on the service elevator. Then you, Miss Jenson, and I will join the others in the lobby, where we will be taken by limos to the marina, and from there by private boat to the island belonging to our esteemed friend, Mr. Kardett." He smiled, like a pleased little elf. "Just think of it! Every member of the jet set can't help but stay in our hotels now that they've been officially sanctioned by Mr. Kardett himself!"

"Shall we go, Mr. Mulvaney?" Julia's voice was bored.

In the lobby, which was actually crowded with people, all beautifully dressed, most of them carrying drinks around, Lori stood uncertainly by the elevator for a moment. The service elevator was located at the very back part of the lobby, off a tiny entryway from the outside.

"Mr. Mulvaney, I'm supposed to meet—"

"I know all about that," he told her, grinning. "Mr. Kardett told me only a short time ago that your plans are for you to meet him in the lounge. However, I believe he's decided not to make it the public lounge. Follow me, please."

"I'm not going to the party," Julia announced. "I plan to spend my entire evening right here in the lobby, Luv, waiting for a call from either my family in London or else from Link, telling me whether or not the sky fell in when he told them about us."

"Not going! But Julia, you love parties like that!"

"Correction, Luv, *did* love parties like that. I went to catch myself a rich husband and, since I'm taken now, by a poor one, unfortunately, there's really no point in my going to those bashes any longer, is there?"

So Julia settled herself in one of the deep soft chairs in the lobby, near the front desk, with a magazine, while Lori let herself be guided by an overeager Michael Mulvaney to a secret lounge, located somewhere on the main floor of the hotel, a sort of VIP place where "important" people could go, be served food or drinks, and not be stared at.

Paul stood facing the fireplace. A small fire had been built there, and the lights in the room were turned off. It was, of course, air-conditioned, so that one had the feeling that it was not a sultry, hot night outside, but that perhaps it was autumn.

"Paul?"

Michael Mulvaney, after holding open the door for Lori, had discreetly closed it again softly.

"You look very beautiful," he said quietly. "Brandy?"

"No, thank you."

He put down his glass and held out both arms. "Come here, little one. You mustn't look so frightened."

She didn't move. She felt . . . uneasy. But she loved

171

him; she knew that for certain. Then why wasn't she happy in his arms, feeling wonderful?

"Lori?"

"Yes," she said finally, and she went to him, leaning against him, her face against his heart. She could hear it, under her cheek. "You've complicated my life," she told him softly.

"Good. That is precisely what I wanted to do. Now why aren't you wearing it?"

"Wearing, oh," Lori said, "the ring. Paul, I couldn't. It's much too—"

"You haven't made up your mind yet, have you?" He looked down at her. As always just looking into his eyes, his face, made her heart beat faster, made her mind seem to hesitate, then slowly change, the way a traveler might pause at a crossroad, then see someone dear and turn down that road after all.

"About leaving?"

"About leaving me."

"All the gifts, the flowers, that expensive ring, Paul, I didn't really want any of those things."

"You're a beautiful woman," he told her quietly, "you deserve those things, and more. I've been thinking about a yacht, something comfortable, so you can live there until I find you a suitable apartment. I need to know the colors you prefer, of course, and the fabrics. I've a friend who owns a boutique in Paris; she could talk with you and—"

"But I don't—"

"I want you to wear the ring," he said. "It's just the color of your eyes."

To leave his arms, to leave that lovely, joyous feeling she got whenever she was this near him, was becoming increasingly difficult. "Paul, I can't accept it, I'm sorry. And all those flowers—" But he was looking absolutely stricken, as if she'd wounded him, abandoned him. "They're all lovely and, and generous of you and I thank you, but—"

"Please," he told her, "let me put the ring on your finger. Do you have it with you?"

He did, gently, sliding it on in a manner that somehow was extremely sensuous. He kissed her finger then, his lips warm, and then, drawing her close to him again, he kissed her mouth. Lori's head was spinning; she would send the flowers to the nearest hospital, give the green robe and shawl and whatever to Julia . . .

But the ring was on her finger, her third finger, left hand, a perfect fit. She offered no resistance when Paul took her hand and led her from the room to his Rolls in the back, settling himself comfortably beside her as they were whisked away.

"Is this the way to the marina?"

"We're taking my seaplane," he told her. "I want some time alone with you at the house, before the others come."

There was no time to talk on the brief, smooth flight to the island. The plane landed on the water and at once they were taken in a speedboat to the island's main dock, where a uniformed butler stood waiting to greet them.

"Is everything in order, Kim?"

"I've a checklist here, sir."

"No," Paul told him, as he took Lori's arm and they began walking up the steps leading to the main house. "I'm sure things are as they should be."

They went on up the steep stone steps to the wide veranda, where flowers had been decked and woven into intricate patterns forming a heart. Inside, in the hallway, white roses formed the shapes of doves in flight; they were all over the downstairs, fragrant, beautiful, those petal-formed birds, some with thin strings of satin ribbon in their flower mouths. At the foot of the huge staircase there was an

173

enormous basket of orchids; a little maid stood by to hand each lady guest an orchid as she went upstairs to the powder room.

All and all it was an out-of-this world party. He took her from room to room, place to place, holding her small hand, his voice warm and enthusiastic as she was introduced to his entire staff of servants, some twenty-seven people, shown the food that was to be served (a fragrant potpourri of vegetables, herbs, spices, and roasting pigeon), then candidly asked her to try the desserts and tell him if they were "perfect."

They were, or nearly so. In fact everything seemed to be, from the freshly waxed and polished floors to the well-run kitchen, now filled with light and lacey cakes with honey and almonds stuffed into their goodness; candied fruit glazed with an exotic sauce made from snails. Every room had vases of expensive flowers; a long bar had been set up in the garden, staffed by servants wearing white silken turbans and starched white serving jackets. From the main fountain, or near it, a dozen musicians were tuning up to play Western music, disco-style. Everything was perfectly organized, luxurious to the point of embarrassment, lovely to look at, exciting to be a part of.

"Lori," Paul said, as they stood on the veranda together, watching the light of the approaching ferryboat get nearer, "do you know why I've done all of this?"

There it was then, the beginning of what it was really all about. He had an odd way of delaying things, putting out props, sending gifts, setting the scene before he talked of important things. Now, now that he had shown her the lavishly decorated house, the exquisite food to be served soon, the wines she'd never heard of to be drunk soon by the guests—now, he seemed ready to talk to her about really vital things, things that, to Lori's way of thinking, were simple and easy to speak of; she loved him. She could make a life for herself without him, however; she was certain of that. She wouldn't die of a broken heart without him because she revered life too much for that, but she knew she loved him, loved him in spite of whatever it was that seemed to be pulling at her, making her uneasy and unhappy, even as he drew her into his arms, there in the fragrant shadows of the veranda, and whispered his words in her ear.

"I did it for you, of course," he told her. "I did it to keep you here." His mouth touched her earlobe. "Do you understand that?"

"I'm not sure—"

"You need be sure of only one thing. That I want you very much."

Want. What about need?

His breath was warm on her throat. "When I realized you would soon be gone, when I knew that there was no time to think, to comprehend what had happened to us, I decided to do the one thing that would keep Mulvaney here."

"Spend money?"

He was taken aback somewhat. "Money is something I never think about."

She was out of his arms now; she'd backed off, and now she stood alone, facing him, looking up into that beautiful, burnished face with the smoldering, sensual dark eyes. "You don't have to think about it, but you always know it's there, and when you want something, when you want your way, you think you need only spend some of it and presto—you'll have what you want!"

He had gone ashen under the deep tan. "What have I done to make you so upset?"

Sudden tears had come to her eyes. "I'm sorry, it's just

that I'm not used to presents and—gifts like this ring—and parties and flowers and—"

"But that's my whole point! I want you to understand that your life will be filled with flowers and gifts! It gives me great pleasure," he said softly, "to have the honor of buying you things, giving you things. I want to see you smile like a child, like a charming child."

She was silent, not answering him. It was as if she was beginning to understand something she had not understood before: With Paul she would always be a kind of child—spoiled, pampered to the extreme. Totally useless.

"I'm not a child," she told him, "I'm a woman. But I don't honestly think you want a woman, Paul. What you want is some kind of delightful person who'll be content to take her pleasure in all the things you buy her, all the Christmas mornings you'll give her. Her position in your life will be, of course, to give you her eternal devotion and loyalty—"

"Why not? Certainly a man can expect that from his mistress, can he not?"

The word seemed to slam itself into her brain, into her heart, so that, for a few seconds, Lori felt actually stunned. Then, very slowly, she turned from her view of the dark spreading sea and looked again at Paul.

"*Mistress.* You haven't explained my duties yet, Paul."

In the near-darkness he couldn't see her face. "Duties? To give me your eternal devotion and loyalty, of course. Look, in case you want me to be honest about it—"

"By all means, do be honest about it!" She was beginning to feel a rising, churning emotion; it boiled inside her, made her eyes moist, filled her throat.

"I didn't ask for this to happen," he said quietly, his face still pale. "I didn't want to have these feelings for you, Lori, and I thought they would surely go away. But they haven't. I dream of you at night, long for you. The thought of you going back to the States made me physically ill, because even if I went to get you and bring you back, I was afraid you'd refuse to come. So I wanted you to see how it would be, if you stayed. How I would deny you nothing. But this angers you." He shook his head. "I'll never understand Western women."

She had to tell him. She just had to.

"You forgot just one thing," she said quietly. "Something that slipped your mind, perhaps. Or maybe it didn't. "Maybe—" she made a sweeping gesture "—all of this is supposed to be come kind of compensation because you're not willing to give me marriage, *to make me your wife!*"

There was a terrible silence between them. Finally Paul turned away and stared out at the black sea.

"I can't do that. There is no point in discussing it. You know the reasons."

"Yes," she said, close to tears, "I know them! A dead girl, a lot of guilt, a lifetime of suffering over something you couldn't help! What you're offering," she told him, her voice thick now, husky with feeling, "what you're offering me, Paul, is dust. Dust and ashes and nothing. A lot of fancy fanfare, a lot of the money you pretend to hate but don't, tossed into the sea, better tossed into the sea, than spent on all of this—this giant, extravagant *lie*—at least in the ocean, the fish could eat the paper!"

"Lori!" He was running after her, chasing her like someone out of a nightmare, finally catching her at the bottom of the stone steps leading to the sea. "Lori, listen to me, will you stop, *you must listen!*"

She took a deep, shaking breath. She would not, she vowed, cry; she would not let him know he could do that, make her cry.

"All right, Paul. Say it, whatever it is you want to say.

And then kindly let me go so I can catch the ferry back to the city when it docks."

He let go of her, his arms dropping at his sides. "I meant no disrespect," he said. "I only meant——"

"No disrespect? What do you think it is when a man asks a girl to be his mistress but never his wife? Or is that supposed to be the difference between the Eastern and the Western world, between your culture and mine?"

"This is a sophisticated world we live in!" Color, red, anger was slowly coming into his face. "It cannot be considered an insult when a man offers to buy a girl whatever she wants because he finds her so beautiful and so desirous that he cannot face life without her!"

"Without having her, you mean! Without making love to her, using her body for——for some kind of escape from your unhappiness!"

"It isn't that."

But it was, and they both knew it, and for a lie to enter into their relationship seemed somehow too ugly to even consider.

"Will you tell your man to please take me back on the boat, Paul?"

"Yes," he said. "Of course." And then, very gently, he traced the outline of her cheek. "It wasn't only that, not totally. It was the feeling I get being near you. Like breathing clean air. Like being with the street children."

She had meant, at some point this evening, when the outrage rose in her like boiling poison, to slap his face. Slap it hard, quickly, and then look at him, into his eyes, to see the shock come into them. It was entirely possible that of all the women who had loved him, he had never been slapped. Even his own mother had never slapped him, most likely, so that certain women probably seemed magical to him, different, enchanted. Lori herself was one of those, one of those whom he seemed bewitched by. To slap him would wake him up, prove that she too had feelings, that he dare not degrade her or insult her as he had done.

Only now, standing there in the moonlight near him, full of tears because of what had happened between them, she knew she could not slap him. In spite of everything that had happened, all the problems, the misunderstandings between them, the other women drifting in and out of their time together, there had been something strong and ever-powerful between them. Whatever it was, it seemed to demand absolute honesty.

"I love you," she said suddenly. "I love you very much and I'll never forget you, Paul. Thank you for making me feel like such a woman!" Suddenly she looked at her hand. Quickly she took off the ring and pressed it into his hand. "It's a beautiful ring. Please keep it to remember us by."

Then she was running, running down the pathway, past the back garden, to the dock where the little ferryboat was unloading its first group of guests, a merry, slightly drunk group that included Michael Mulvaney.

If he were to see her there would be necessary explanations; she would have to explain why she wasn't going to be at the party, what she'd been doing here before anybody else, and so forth.

There was a small, open summerhouse not far from the boat deck, a shadowy hundred or so yards from the place where everybody got off the boat. The little captain, if that's what he was, seemed in no hurry to leave at once; he stood around talking with some of the men, British TV people, along with an American newscaster, a woman, sent to cover the extravaganza. There would be plenty of time to get back to the dock and go across to shore when he left to bring back more guests.

Almost without wanting to Lori looked toward the great,

179

sprawling house. She remembered very well which room on the second floor was Paul's; it was the center one, with the balcony.

As she watched, blazing lights suddenly filled that part of the house, and seconds later, as Lori stood transfixed, the balcony door burst open. In the moonlight the two figures took on a kind of silvery glow.

It was Paul, of course; his body was etched on her mind, in her heart, forever. It was Paul who started to go back inside, but the woman stopped him, reaching out, her long hair flinging itself in front of her face for a second. But she had caught him by the shoulder and now she pointed a finger at him; as he turned away, she followed him back inside.

The woman was Jasmine, the dancer.

Twelve

The lobby of the Alexandria Teresa was deserted, except for a petulant young man behind the desk, annoyed that he didn't get to go to the biggest party of the decade, and for Julia, who sat dozing, her feet curled up under her, her head resting on the arm of a large, overstuffed chair.

"Hello," Lori said, giving her friend a slight shake. "I'm back. You knew I would be, didn't you?"

Julia stared at Lori with level blue eyes. "He didn't then, did he?"

They began going toward the glass elevator. "He didn't do a lot of things. He didn't say one word about our future, except to promise me a lot of things. And he didn't . . . I don't remember him saying he loved me. Only that he wanted me."

The sliding door closed and instantly they were being rushed upward.

"This thing always leaves my stomach down there someplace," Julia said, closing her eyes. She was silent until they'd reached their floor. "I can, I assume, say with confidence that the gentleman did not ask you to marry him, along with all the other things he didn't do. Am I right?"

"I'd rather not talk about it."

"See here," Julia said, fumbling for the room key in her large handbag. "In case it hasn't occurred to you, Duckie, I really am off for London tonight. I'll only be going that far with the rest of you, and we won't get a bloody chance to talk on the flight, you can bet. The rest of the group is going on to Paris, and they'll start partying for that long before London. So if you've something important to say, best say it very soon."

"I told you," Lori said, going at once to the dressing table, beginning to take down her hair, which she'd pinned high on her head. With a kind of vengeance she yanked out the pins, shaking her head until her hair fell around her shoulders, tumbled down her back. "I don't want to talk about it."

"Very well then; I'll just say toodle-oo right now and get the first commercial flight out to London, instead of waiting to go with—"

"Julia, you wouldn't!"

"If I'm not being of any help here, why shouldn't I go on to London to be with Link? Lord knows my family is probably giving him a hard time at this very moment, poor thing."

Lori carefully put down the hairbrush. "All right, then. He—he wanted me to be his mistress."

"He *what*?"

Lori nodded, feelings of anger and misery making her voice uneven. "He wanted to set me up in—in an apartment and buy me a lot of things. That was the life he had decided he was going to offer me."

"I hope you let him know in no uncertain terms that a rich man who doesn't marry a girl is like borrowing somebody else's diamond ring! It's got to be marriage or nothing!"

Lori couldn't help but smile. "It wasn't the things he bought me, Julia. What on earth would a girl do with twelve dozen roses every single day?"

"I've an uncle in London who'd back-sell them on the streets."

"There's something else," Lori said quietly. "Something that's been bothering me ever since I went to visit Stephanie." She looked at Julia in the glass. "Even if he had asked me to be his wife, that wouldn't have changed the way he'd want me to live, the way he'd want me to *be*!" She suddenly realized what a caring friend Julia really was. "You understood that before I did, didn't you? You knew I'd never be happy sitting around at some swank resort trying to figure out what to wear to the next party! Even having Paul beside me wouldn't change that! I need—I've got to have more in my life than that! Otherwise I just become some sort of, of possession of Paul's, someone he likes to dress up and look at and be in love with. But unless I'm myself . . ."

But who was this self? Was it the shy little girl from Chicago whose dreams died when her young fiancé was killed? Or was it perhaps the saddened, quiet-spoken young woman Paul had been attracted to? Or had she really been neither of those, but someone else, someone able and willing to reach out to others with love, so that her love didn't only center on her man but reached out to the world, to everyone near her who needed kindness and understanding and help.

"I'm coming back, you know," she told Julia suddenly. "I'm going home and I'm going to talk things over with my parents; this one time they just might be able to understand my real feelings. But I'm coming back."

The worried look had come again into Julia's eyes. "Do you mean to tell me that once you're safely back home again, you're going to turn around and come back here? You have no visa—"

"My friend at the hospital will help me with that, I'm sure."

Julia's eyes widened. "So that's it. That's what it's all about."

"They need help there, Julia. I can run errands and—and write letters for patients and do whatever I'm told. But the point is I'll be doing something important."

Julia was at the balcony, looking down at the street. "Since you don't seem to think merely standing around giving solace and comfort to Paul Kardett is what you want to do with your life, maybe you'd better tell him that. He just drove up like a madman and parked his car with half of it sticking out in the street!"

Lori's face went pale. "I didn't tell you all of it. I didn't tell you that all the time he was asking me to be his mistress, another girl was right there in his house, living there! I saw them together, after I'd left him, she came out onto a balcony with him."

"Lori, are you ever going to learn that he probably sees nothing at all wrong with having a lot of women around him all the time? He wasn't born in your good old American Chicago, you know. He comes from a culture quite different from yours and mine." Julia closed the balcony doors. "Go and hear him out, Luv. After all, in spite of everything that's wrong with him, you're still very much in love with him, aren't you?"

"Yes," Lori said quietly. "Unfortunately."

"Very well then, go and speak to him before he jumps off a mountain or something!"

When she got off the elevator, the desk clerk hurried to her to tell her Mr. Kardett was waiting for her in the garden. He wasn't; he was on the small veranda overlooking Michael Mulvaney's version of the water fountains at Versailles: sprays of lavender and pink lights under water, making a rather gaudy display.

"You're a very rude girl," he said, as soon as Lori appeared at the doors. "Has anyone ever told you that?"

The impact of his physical presence, the nearness of him there by her, made Lori feel somehow changed, different. Seeing him always did that to her. That is being in love, she told herself sternly. Like an illness, it affects one's thinking processes!

"I suppose I was rude, running off like that," she told him. "I'm sorry."

"How sorry?"

She let her breath out. "As sorry as good manners dictate, Paul. Look, you ought to be very glad I didn't push you into the fountain or something!"

He began to smile at her, a slow, white, extremely charming grin.

"You can push me now," he said. "Go ahead!"

"Paul, I don't like your coming here, following me this way!" She leaned against the railing, her pretty dress crushing against her. "I gave you my answer."

"Yes, but what was the question?"

Games. Well, wasn't that actually his life, some sort of game he played, going places, getting in and out of planes, jets, boats, trains, whatever, going places, buying things, spending money on people, giving money away—always running from his rage and grief and terrible, heartbreaking guilt?

"The question," she said, her voice low, "was whether or not I wanted to spend my time sitting around in some beautiful apartment waiting for you to call. Or when you were busy with someone else would you expect me to merely sit back and wait and spend more of your money while doing it?"

"Busy with—" He looked at her, his eyes deepening. "So it's true; you do love me. You are jealous!"

"I am not! Just because I happened to, to see you and Jasmine on the balcony, that doesn't mean—"

"You are jealous."

"And even if I am," she said, beginning to wish she hadn't given in and come running the way she'd done, "it has nothing to do with what we're talking about."

"That was Jasmine you saw," he told her matter-of-factly, almost as if that should settle the matter once and for all.

"Yes; I know it was. And I wasn't spying on you, if that's what you think."

The smile again. "Of course you weren't. But for your information she happens to be Betha's sister. Or did you know that, perhaps?"

She hadn't, but it didn't matter. Somehow the idea of having his dead lover's sister living in his house—

"I really am not interested in discussing your love problems, Paul," she told him. She desperately wanted to run, to run until she sank to, into, the ground. Odd, when people hurt other people, the best way to handle it is not to let them know they are wounding you. "I have packing to do. I don't think Mr. Mulvaney is going to let even a mass hangover deter him any longer."

"She's a friend. No; really she is that and only that. Do you think I'm the kind of man who cannot have a woman for a friend only?"

"I simply can't imagine that, frankly."

"She wants to help me." His eyes were serious. "All the time she is telling me to stop my grief, to let it go from myself. And when she saw me after I had been with you, she knew you were to be my happiness."

He was going on, she realized, as if he didn't hear her, didn't care what she'd told him before, and wasn't interested in what she was saying now.

"I must say good-bye now," she told him. She hated good-byes; she never should have come here to meet him, just because he'd followed her, driven and parked his car like a madman.

"First, another question." He reached out and brought her to him.

"No, no more questions! No—more—anything!"

But his mouth was very close to hers.

"Marry me, Lori! I want to marry you."

She had not guessed, ever, what the impact of those words would be, what they would do to her, mean to her. For a moment it was as if bells really did ring; the angels really did dance in sheer joy and all was well in her world. Then, and only when she had taken that first, joyous peek at what Paul was promising, offering her, was she able to reject it.

"That's very sweet of you to say that."

"Sweet? What the devil is sweet? I'm asking you to be my wife; I'm telling you I want to take you to Jerusalem, near where my parents were married, and I want to marry you there. I want . . ."

There was that word again: *want*. What about *need*, what about his *need for her*?

There was no use talking about it. He was, as she'd been warned, educated in the manner of the British aristocracy, but at heart he remained an Eastern man, steeped in their traditions and customs and habits.

Lori put out her hand.

"Good-bye."

"Why should I tell you good-bye when you are not going someplace? There's no need," he said earnestly, "for us to be apart, now that I understand that I offended you by not offering to marry you at once. But to tell you the truth, it was not possible then. I'm very surprised that it is even possible now, for me to propose marriage."

"Well," Lori told him, "it's very flattering to be proposed to by someone who can buy me whatever I want, whenever I want it, I suppose, but it isn't enough, you see."

He smiled at her. "If you despise all the luxury, I will buy you a farm, with rivers and streams and roses growing wild. There we can take long walks in the moonlight—"

"Tell me, Paul, how often do you propose to come home? I mean, how long would your businesses and holdings and ships keep you away?"

"How long? Why, as long as it takes."

"And in the meantime what would I do? Hang around with your rich, beach-bum buddies who have private beaches and private planes and public miseries? No, thank you." She started to leave him, but at the glass doors, she paused.

"Paul, what does *shalom* mean?"

He looked bleak, lost, friendless, standing there alone in the circle of moonlight.

187

"Recompense. Why do you ask me that?"

"It's a beautiful word," she told him softly. "And I'm glad it doesn't mean good-bye."

She would not, would not cry—not until she was upstairs and in the room and in a sisterly embrace with a very kind and understanding Julia.

And so there was nothing left to do now, the livelong day, but finish packing and pretend to be busy and sit through the last staff meeting before Paris, and finally have a light meal with Julia in the dining room, along with a jovial Mr. Mulvaney and a beaming Frank Corita, who had received a cablegram saying his daughter had given birth to twin boys, one of whom had been named Frank and the other Joseph Frank. Nothing left to do but try to push the thought of life without him from her mind. There was, however, a blessed, easy answer, so sweet and simple that she wondered why she hadn't thought of that during the hardest, heaviest part of her grieving for Tommy. The answer was not to stifle, to try to destroy her natural feelings of love, but to let them out, to open the cage and let them come out and in holding out her arms to the world around her, her own feeling of emptiness would surely vanish after due time.

The best place to practice this newfound wisdom was at the Good Shepherd Hospital, observing Stephanie's love for people, seeing it put into action. There she could become the girl she needed to be, sane and loving and dependable, able to give right on through her own sad and lonely times, able to hold out her hand and tell a joke even though there would be flashes of his face, coming across her mind as if they'd been projected: Paul smiling, his eyes dark and warm, laughing at something she'd said, his head thrown back, his strong throat showing little ropes that throbbed whenever he was aroused. . . .

"—and so, one and all," Mr. Mulvaney said at the final banquet dinner, "we raise our glasses to salute one of the most mysterious and romantic cities in the world— *Alexandria!*"

"Did you hear what the man said, Luv?" It was Julia, leaning toward her at the banquet table, whispering. "The cars are waiting out in front now. We've only to fetch our bags and we'll be off and flying home."

"Yes," Lori said woodenly, "I heard." I will come back, she told herself firmly. I won't let them keep me from coming back! But there was a chance, of course, that she wouldn't, that once home the routine would settle in and her parents' disapproval would rise and finally, finally, she would decide no, it had all been a lovely, lovely dream— the city and her friends here—and Paul.

She had a few last moments alone, in the bedroom, just before leaving the hotel for the airport. There was always that certain perfume hanging over the city, mingled, carried on the sea air. Lori went out on the balcony and looked once again at the lights.

There was a pounding at the door. "Ready, Luv? Let's bloody well get out of this creepy place!"

She sat next to Julia in the limo, between Mr. Mulvaney and Frank Corita. They had left the wide highway, with groves of grapes and fruit trees on either side, far behind, and now, the road was more narrow and beyond there were rising brown hills. Michael Mulvaney had started singing French songs from World War I, and Julia looked at Lori and winked.

It was not long after he had finished "Mademoiselle from Armentières" for the second time that they noticed the car. It was a small green sports car of some sort, topless, going very fast, gaining on them, as a matter of fact.

Julia, there beside Lori, had twisted around in her seat to look out the back window. Suddenly she grabbed Lori's shoulder convulsively.

"Isn't that one of Paul's cars, Lori?"

Lori turned around in time to see the small car jerk forward, going at a frightening rate now. For an instant she thought he was going to pass them, there on the narrow road, but he didn't; he came up next to them, driving abreast with them. He had begun making jabbing motions of a sort, then pointing at Lori.

"Lori, will you please do something to stop him, before he kills us all?"

Michael Mulvaney was hammering wildly on the glass separating them from the chauffeur, Frank Corita was yelling something out the open window, shaking his fist at Paul, and both cars were still doing eighty-five. One of the tires began making a strange, hissing sound.

"If I remember correctly," Julia said, "there's a bridge up here, and there won't be room enough for both cars. So if you'll excuse me, I'm bailing out!"

"Julia, no!" Lori looked desperately at the green car. Paul didn't seem to be watching the road at all; he drove with one hand and used the other to point and otherwise make sign language.

Finally, mercifully, only a hundred or so feet from the bridge, the limo pulled over and everybody inside breathed a sigh of relief.

In an instant Paul's car had skidded to a stop; he ran over, jerked open the limo door, and stuck his head inside. He was glaring.

"You aren't leaving," he said grimly.

Michael Mulvaney sat up straighter. "Now see here—"

"It's all right," Lori said quickly, half-stumbling over Julia's feet. "I'll meet all of you at the airport. I promise."

"But does *he* promise?" It was Frank Corita, beginning to get red in the face.

"I have something to tell the lady that will only take seconds," Paul said quietly. "I am not kidnapping her. Please go on and we will follow."

She allowed herself to be led to his car. She got in, folded her hands, and silently told her heart to kindly not hammer that way.

"I think you'd better explain," she told him, as he started the car.

"It's very simple." He looked at her; he was obviously pleased to see her sitting there close to him. "I thought about the word you asked me about. Do you remember?"

"Shalom?"

"Yes, shalom. Remember I told you it means recompense?"

"Paul—"

"And it came to me as I was driving back to the marina today that when that word came into your mind it came for a reason. It was a message."

"A message!"

"Of course," he said, covering her hand with his. "I have suffered much, had a great loss, and you are my recompense. With you I can begin again." He held her hand to his warm mouth. "And the same with you, you see. So we are meant for each other; our union has already been decided. Do you understand?"

"Paul, I wouldn't be happy just being the wife of a rich man, doing nothing."

"Then do whatever you like."

She looked at him. "What did you say?"

"I said, little flower, do whatever you like. I have no wish to change you and make you like some of those other women who have become very unwomanly."

"Then you won't mind if I'm gone, working at the hospital for long hours?"

"Of course not. I shall consider the lilies and meet with the street children to ponder out life's many secrets."

She was smiling now, feeling higher and higher on joy.

"And will you help rebuild Stephanie's burned-out hospital?"

"I will see that all my street children are taken there whenever they need to have their tonsils taken from them."

She hugged him impulsively.

"In return I'll never be jealous again, I promise!"

"Good. Because Jasmine is very worried about all of this and wants very much to be your friend."

She put her hand on his arm. "And Betha?"

"A sweet memory I have put away."

So it was all well; she need not grieve any longer. The car sped on toward Jerusalem and the border, toward the wall and the old city.

"But we promised we'd meet everybody in Cairo at the airport!"

"And so we will," he told her. "But first put on the ring, please."

He handed her the box. Inside was the stunning emerald, but this time it had company. There was a wedding band next to it.

"First we get married," he told her. "Then we get the ring inscribed."

She didn't have to ask him the word, or why. It was, of course, already inscribed on her heart!

Shalom.